THE MAN WHO
SAW HER BEAUTY

THE MAN WHO
SAW HER BEAUTY

BY

MICHELLE DOUGLAS

First published in Great Britain 2012
by Mills & Boon, an imprint of Harlequin (UK) Limited.
Large Print edition 2012
Harlequin (UK) Limited, Eton House,
18-24 Paradise Road, Richmond, Surrey TW9 1SR

© Michelle Douglas 2012

ISBN: 978 0 263 22604 1

Harlequin (UK) policy is to use papers that are natural,
renewable and recyclable products and made from
wood grown in sustainable forests. The logging and
manufacturing process conform to the legal environmental
regulations of the country of origin.

Printed and bound in Great Britain
by CPI Antony Rowe, Chippenham, Wiltshire

For Pa, with love.

CHAPTER ONE

BLAIR peered into the mirror with the kind of fierce concentration she normally reserved for casting judgement on her Blair Mac designs for Spring Fashion Week. She didn't take in her entire face. She fixed only on her left eye.

She held it wide and very carefully attached the false eyelashes. She blinked. She repeated the procedure for her right eye. As a model, she'd learned how to do this twenty years ago. She hadn't expected to need it now she was no longer in front of a camera or parading down a catwalk, though.

It just goes to show.

Next she attached the false eyebrows. That was a newly acquired skill. Unlike the lashes, they wouldn't need to be removed every day. If she took care they should remain in place for several weeks.

Her eyebrows had always been fair, but full. She'd used to get them tinted.

Once upon a time.

She pushed the thought away. No point mooning about the past.

She reached for the wig, removed it carefully from its stand and ran a hand down the long length of blonde synthetic hair. Even a trained eye would find it hard to tell the difference between this wig and her old hair. Her friend Dana, hairdresser extraordinaire, had warned her that the wig was too long, but Blair had chosen it anyway. She'd found comfort in the fact that it looked so much like her old hair.

She pulled the wig on over her scalp, tugged it into place, and then turned back to the mirror to make whatever adjustments were necessary. Adjustments that would help her look normal. Adjustments that would help her look whole and healthy. Adjustments that would hopefully ensure people started treating her like a fully functioning adult again.

Finally she stepped back and viewed her face in its entirety. She reached for her pot of blusher. More colour on her cheeks wouldn't go amiss. She applied another coat of tawny-pink lipstick with its advertised stay-put power, and once again gave thanks for the skills she'd learned as a model.

She stepped back again, viewed her face—first

from the left side and then the right—and then nodded at her reflection. Her heartbeat slowed. Finally she could recognise herself. When she ventured outside today no one would be able to tell.

And no one was here now to see the way her hand shook as she capped her lipstick, or the trouble she had screwing the lid back on to the pot of blusher.

You have a lot to give thanks for. Chin up!

She averted her gaze from the mirror as she undid her wrap. She snapped her bra and prosthesis into place and pulled a T-shirt on over her head as quickly as she could.

Problem was, she reflected as she tugged on her jeans, it wasn't gratitude that was in her heart. It was fear. Fear that life would never feel normal again. Fear that Glory would never stop fussing, would never stop being afraid for her. Fear that her beloved aunt would worry herself into an early grave.

Glory was talking about selling up and moving to Sydney to be closer to her! Blair dropped to the bed and pulled on her boots. Glory had lived here in Dungog her entire life. She'd hate the city.

Blair glanced at the mirror again. She put a hand under her chin to physically lift it higher. She owed Glory everything. She had to put her aunt's mind at rest. She *had* to. That was why she'd come home. Blair was out of danger. She *was* healthy again. Once Glory realised that...

She leapt up to toss her cosmetics into her make-up bag. The make-up bag she took everywhere. Just in case. For touch ups. Emergencies. Once she'd succeeded in convincing Glory she was better... Well, then they could all get back to normality.

And that was what she really wanted—normality. Her motives weren't purely altruistic.

She paused to grip her hands in front of her. Bluff. That was the answer. If she could bluff her way into winning the Miss Showgirl quest twenty years ago, bluff her way into a modelling career and then bluff her way into fashion college, surely she could bluff everyone into thinking she was healthy again?

She pulled in a breath. 'Piece of cake.' The mirror proved that she could still present herself to the best possible advantage. Looking at her, nobody would believe that she was anything but healthy and whole.

You are healthy.

* * *

'Oh, Blair, look at you!' Glory said the moment Blair entered the kitchen. 'You look fabulous. As if...'

'As if I'd never been sick,' Blair finished for her.

'Well, yes, but...'

Bluff! She twirled on the spot for good effect. 'I'm as good as new.' She kissed her aunt on the cheek before taking her seat and pouring muesli into a bowl. Bluff had not got her through surgery and chemotherapy. Glory had done that.

'Tea?' Glory lifted the teapot.

'Yes, please. And stop looking at me like that, Aunt Glory. The last few months have been... hard.'

'Hell on earth,' Glory growled.

She reached across to clasp her aunt's hand. 'And it's beyond wonderful to have the opportunity to spend a month mooching around here. I can't tell you how much I've been looking forward to it.'

'I can't tell you how good it is to have you home.'

Glory's bottom lip quivered and Blair wanted to kick herself all over again for going back to work so soon, for fainting, for worrying everyone anew. She knew how much her aunt loved her. She knew how much her aunt had feared losing her. She knew what her aunt had gone through.

It was why she'd given herself this month off as a holiday.

She swallowed the hard knot in her throat. 'Aunt Glory, they got all the cancer. They blasted me with chemo to make sure. I'm getting stronger every day. I'm practically as healthy as any other woman my age. I'm going to live a long and fulfilling life. No more kid gloves, okay? It's time for things to get back to normal.'

'No more kid gloves?' Glory murmured, but she shook her head as she said it.

'That's right. So drink your tea before it gets cold.'

Blair waited until her aunt had eaten a piece of toast before saying, 'You said last night that you have a meeting of the Agricultural Show Society today?'

'Ooh, yes.'

The enthusiasm in Glory's voice gladdened Blair's heart. 'With the show in three months' time, I'm guessing this is the first official planning meeting?'

'That's right, love, and everyone will be there.'

'Fabulous! Count me in.'

Her aunt's teaspoon clattered back to its saucer. 'Oh, but, Blair…'

She tried not to wince at the anxiety that strained her aunt's voice. She'd lain awake last night, thinking of ways she could prove to Glory that she was okay again. Being seen out and about in the community, and functioning fully and normally was the best she'd been able to come up with. 'It'll be lovely to catch up with people I haven't seen in a while. And surely there'll be some small thing or two that I can help out with for the next month or so?'

'You should be resting!'

'Oh, I'll be doing plenty of that too.' She stretched her arms back behind her and grinned. 'I'm on holiday—I plan on being lazy and having some fun. The show-planning will be fun. I always loved this time of year when I was a girl.'

'I remember.'

The wistful note in Glory's voice had Blair's throat thickening all over again.

The show meeting was every bit as gruelling as Blair had expected.

There were all the expected stares that made her flinch and cringe inside, and lots of 'My, aren't you looking well?' comments, and genuine surprise that helped ease all that flinching and cringing. She had no intention of being an object of pity.

Oh, poor Blair. It's so terrible to lose your parents at such a young age.

She'd grown up with that refrain and she'd hated it. There was no way she was adding, *Oh, poor Blair. It's terrible to lose a breast so young*, to the litany.

Even if it *was* terrible.

Even if she couldn't look at herself in the mirror naked any more.

Nobody else needed to know that.

So she chatted and laughed, drank tea and ate cake, and took a seat at the table when Joan, the chair of the Agricultural Show Society, called the meeting to order. She listened intently as the meeting progressed, and even made an occasional suggestion.

'Rightio—let's move on to…' Joan checked the agenda '…the Miss Showgirl quest.'

Blair shifted on her seat. The Dungog Miss Showgirl quest was part-beauty-pageant, part-charity-fundraiser, and part-public-speaking contest, and had been part of the town's history for as long as anyone could remember.

And twenty years ago *she'd* won it.

Perspiration prickled her scalp as inevitable comparisons bombarded her. Her body had been perfect once, and she'd never fully appreciated it. Now, it was…

She swallowed and blinked hard. She didn't want to remember how perfect her body had been twenty years ago and how imperfect it was now. Her hands clenched against the assault of grief. She didn't want to be reminded of all she'd lost. She risked a glance at Glory. Could she sneak out of the meeting unobserved?

As if sensing Blair's pain, Glory swung round.

Blair schooled her features. 'Ooh, what fun!' She rubbed her hands together. 'How many contestants are there this year?'

'Girls?' Joan called down to the end of the table where a group of teenage girls were gathered. 'How many of you are entering for the quest?' She counted the raised hands. 'Ten? Lovely.'

There'd been a dozen in Blair's year.

'Now, we do have a bit of a problem.'

Aware of her aunt's gaze, still surveying her from the other side of the table, Blair kept her face clear and her attention squarely on Joan.

'Lexxie Hamilton, who is normally mentor to the contestants, is unfortunately unable to take up the role this year. So we are going to need a new mentor. Would anyone like to volunteer for the role…or put someone's name forward as a suggestion?'

Nobody said anything.

Joan turned to Blair. 'Blair, honey, for how long are you in town?'

Out of the corner of her eye she saw her aunt shake her head at Joan. She pushed her shoulders back. 'I'm here for a whole month and I would love to help out.' She was aware of Glory stiffening and shaking her head again, and of Joan's gaze flicking to Glory before moving back to Blair. She lifted her chin and smiled brightly. 'I would *love* to be the Miss Showgirl mentor for the next month.'

Joan cleared her throat. 'We should hate to put you out, Blair. We all know what you've been through—'

'Put me out?' She snorted, and then deliberately beamed at Glory. 'From memory, I meet with the showgirl entrants for two hours a week, yes? That's not putting me out at all. It'll be fun.'

Glory bit her lip. 'Fun?'

'You bet.' While she had control of the floor she glanced to where the entrants sat. 'Do Thursday nights—six-thirty till eight-thirty—suit everyone?' Ten hands instantly shot into the air. 'There—done! And that gives you a whole month to find a replacement for when I go back to the city.'

Joan glanced at Glory again. 'Well… I…'

Blair smiled at her aunt with deliberate blitheness, as if unaware of her aunt's objections, effectively preventing Glory from shaking her head at Joan again.

'Um…thank you, Blair. That will be a great help.'

'Blair, honey?' Glory caught up with Blair at the refreshments table after the meeting had ended. 'I'm going to be held up here for another couple of hours. You must be tired. Why don't you go on home ahead of me?'

'I'm not tired.' The denial sprang from Blair automatically. She immediately tempered it with, 'But I wouldn't mind dropping by the newsagent's and grabbing a couple of fashion magazines. I think I need to swot up.'

Glory huffed out a sigh. 'I'm vexed with Joan for putting you on the spot like that. Are you sure you really want to take on the role of mentor? I can have a word with her and—'

'Not at all! I'm looking forward to being involved.'

'But you're on holiday! I don't want you overdoing things.'

Like she had when she'd gone back to work too early? She seized a plate and loaded it with a couple of small triangle sandwiches and piece of sultana cake. 'Aunt Glory, I've learned my lesson. I promise. Besides, two hours a week is hardly going to be overdoing anything.'

'Well…I guess not.'

'And you're more than welcome to join in the fun as assistant mentor.'

'Me?' Glory blinked. 'What on earth do I know about fashion? You know I never understood it. I sent you to school either with skirts too long or too short. And if ankle socks were in I'd buy you knee-high or vice versa.'

Blair laughed. Really laughed. And she couldn't remember the last time in three or four months when that had happened. 'I loved growing up with you, Aunt Glory. You know that.'

'Yes, I do. But a fashion expert…'

'You're not,' Blair finished for her.

'Those girls are lucky to have you. Promise me you won't overdo it.'

'I promise. Now, I don't want *you* overdoing things either. You've hardly eaten a thing all day. I'm not leaving until you've had a cup of tea and eaten that.'

She handed her surprised aunt the plate, poured her a cup of tea and proceeded to outline her plans for the Miss Showgirl meetings. 'We'll talk hair and make-up and clothes and deportment and all good things—what could be more fun than that?'

Fun? She had to bite back hysterical laughter. Hair and make-up weren't fun for her any more. They were essential tools that stopped people staring at her, pitying her. Hair and make-up stopped her looking like a freak.

'You always did have a knack for those things,' Glory allowed. She eyed her niece, setting down her now empty plate. 'Fun, you say?'

She pasted on her brightest smile. 'Absolutely.' She hugged her aunt and then wished she hadn't as the prosthesis that was now masquerading as her right breast pressed again the scar tissue of her chest, reminding her afresh of all the ways she'd changed. 'It looks like your next meeting is about to start. I'll leave you to it and see you back home.'

She set off towards the back entrance of the showground office building, reminding herself that Rome hadn't been built in a day. It would take more than a day to quieten all of Glory's fears.

As she neared the door voices drifted in from outside. Her steps slowed. She obviously wasn't the only one using this particular shortcut to access the nearest side street. She hesitated, but only for a moment. She might be all socialised out and ready—make that more than ready—for some downtime, but she hadn't come back to Dungog to go into hibernation. She forced her feet towards the wide double doors—one of which was closed.

'You are going to make such a fool of yourself, Stevie Conway, so don't say you weren't warned! You know you're not pretty enough to be Miss Showgirl. Our advice...' A collection of titters salted the air and brought Blair up short. 'Quit now while you still can, before you become a laughing stock!'

Blair saw red. In an instant. And the red of anger felt fantastic after the blacks and greys of fear.

With a flash of strength she thrust the heavy wooden door open so hard that it banged against the wall behind. Four girls at the bottom of the stairs spun to face her.

'I want each and every one of you girls to listen to me very carefully.'

She strode down the steps, there were eleven of them, and used her catwalk stride—a high lift of her knees, a sway of her hips, and a haughty angle to her chin—to ensure that she had their complete attention. She stopped one step short to maintain the height advantage. She deliberately placed her hands on her hips to look as big as she could; she leant forward so it would appear to them as if she loomed.

'Miss Showgirl is not some trifling beauty pageant. It's about learning life-enhancing skills that will take you forward in life while raising money for a worthwhile cause. It's about learning to make the most of yourselves—physically, spiritually, *and* intellectually.'

Nobody said anything. Instead of feeling helpless and feeble, just for a moment Blair felt powerful again. And that was beyond fantastic.

'I wasn't the prettiest entrant the year I won. Go back and look at the photographs. Monica Dalwood was.' Monica had been a gorgeous redhead with a crippling shyness she hadn't been able to master.

She met and held each girl's gaze. It took her less than five seconds to work out which of them was Stevie Conway, and it wasn't because Stevie wasn't pretty. She was. She was lovely. She was also an archetypal tomboy—jeans, short-cropped hair, not a scrap of make-up or a single item of jewellery in sight. She made a complete contrast to her three rivals.

Blair pushed her shoulders back. 'If the only thing you girls are interested in is who's the fairest in all the land, then I'll give you a score out of ten now.'

She'd give each of them ten out of ten. She could see, though, that her assertion disconcerted them. They didn't like being judged on their looks alone and the discovery pleased her.

'But if you choose to know the score then know this—I will not accept you into my Thursday evening meetings. So, girls, what's it to be?'

There was a round of murmured 'Thursday evenings, miss.'

'Good. Now, one final thing. If I ever hear any of you make a comment like the one I heard as I was coming out through that door then we will have serious words—understand?'

Nods all around.

'Excellent.' She dusted off her hands. 'Now, I'm sure you ladies have much better things to do than hang around here all day.'

They didn't need any further encouragement. Three of the girls shot off in one direction. Stevie took off in the other.

'Stevie, wait.'

Stevie stopped, stiffened, and then whirled around. 'You heard it all, didn't you? And you know I'm Stevie because I'm not as pretty as they are.' She waved a hand in the direction the three other girls had gone.

'I didn't hear it all,' Blair countered, 'but I certainly heard enough. And I know you're Stevie because you're walking on your own while the others took off together.'

The younger girl's shoulders unhitched a fraction.

'I really hope you didn't pay any attention to what those girls said. You have as good a chance of being Miss Showgirl as they have.'

'It's not true, though, is it? Not even my dad thinks I have a fighting chance of winning!'

It took all of Blair's strength to prevent her jaw from dropping. Any father worth his salt would be trying to build his daughter's confidence, not undermining it.

Stevie flung an arm in the air. 'No matter how hard I try, I'll never be able to look like those other girls.'

'Good Lord, why would you want to?'

She was rewarded when Stevie's chin shot up. 'What?'

She held up a finger. 'When you are speaking in public or being interviewed it's always: *I beg your pardon*. Not, *What*. And, sure, those girls who were teasing you are pretty, but they're blonde clones. It's hard to tell them apart.'

Stevie choked. 'You're not allowed to say that.'

'Why not?' Blair steered them towards the gate in the fence. 'I'm blonde, and some would say pretty, but believe me, if you saw me first thing in the morning before I'd had a chance to fix my hair and make-up you'd get a right fright.'

Wasn't that the truth!

Exactly how true it was had nausea rising up through her. She swallowed it back. 'You work with what you have, and, Stevie, you have a lot— the most wonderful olive skin and gorgeous hair.'

Stevie's hair might be short, but it was shiny and dark, and full and thick. 'Your eyes are the most amazing colour.' Blue-grey. 'Miss Showgirl will be awarded to the contestant who stands out, who proves herself. It won't go to blonde clones the judges can't tell apart.'

Stevie thought about that for a moment. 'But if one of the blonde clones can make herself stand out, if she proves herself...'

'If she's worked that hard,' Blair said gently, ushering Stevie through the gate, 'then she might deserve to win.'

Stevie stopped. Blair stopped too. 'You really, truly think I have a chance and you're not just saying that because you're our mentor and that's what you're supposed to say?'

'I really, truly mean it.' Blair crossed her heart. Then she frowned. 'Is winning that important to you?'

The younger girl shook her head. 'I just want to know that I have as good a chance as the others, that's all.'

She sensed there was more. 'And?'

'Sometimes I want to be...just more than jeans and T-shirts!' she burst out. 'My mum died when I was little so I don't have anyone to show me how to do all that girly stuff, and when I try I just look stupid!'

No mother? And a father who didn't think she was pretty? Blair's heart started to throb for this lovely girl. 'Scarves,' she suddenly pronounced.

'Wha—? I beg your pardon?'

'I don't think frills and lots of jewellery are your kind of thing, Stevie. You'd probably find them too fussy. But you can add the most gorgeous feminine touch by using a scarf. And if you wake up in the morning and don't feel like doing feminine you can change the scarf to something funky or something classic instead. With your lovely cheekbones and long throat you'd look great in a scarf. I'll do a class on them.'

Stevie stared. 'Really?' she breathed.

Something inside Blair's chest flickered. 'Sure, why not?'

Stevie continued to stare as if Blair had just given her the secret to the universe. Blair cleared her throat, suddenly self-conscious. 'Stevie, you want to know my secret?'

The younger girl leant forward, suddenly eager. 'You mean your secret to winning Miss Showgirl?' she breathed.

Blair nodded. 'Bluff.'

Stevie's face fell. 'Bluff?'

'Pretending, play-acting, fooling everyone into believing what you want them to believe—that you're smart and pretty and confident. If you act like you think you're pretty and smart and have something to offer the world, if you walk and talk and meet people's stares head-on with that kind of confidence and belief in yourself, they'll start to see that you really are something special. And they'll treat you with respect. It's not easy to begin with,' she warned. 'It's really, really hard. But it works. And eventually you'll realise that you're not pretending any more. You'll discover that you really are pretty and smart and confident.'

And then, sometimes, something happens that takes it all from you again.

She tried not to flinch at that thought. She tried to banish it to a place where it couldn't batter her shattered self-esteem further.

'Bluff?' Stevie said as if testing the word out.

Blair lifted her chin and squared her shoulders. 'Bluff.' And if she said it a little too strongly then so be it. 'So, will I see you on Thursday?'

Nick slammed his brakes on the moment he saw Stevie. He pulled the car over to the side of the road. What on earth...? She'd told him she was spending the day baking with her best friend Poppy and Poppy's mother.

So what was his daughter doing here at the exit to the showground, talking to some woman he'd never seen before?

The showground...?

The Miss Showgirl quest?

Nick bit back a groan and rested his head against the steering wheel for a moment before pushing himself out of the car. He dragged a breath into a chest that hurt. 'Stevie?'

Stevie spun around and her face fell. Almost comically, he noted, only he didn't feel the least like laughing. Her chin shot up as he drew near. 'Hey, Dad.'

She said it as if nothing were amiss, but he sensed her defensiveness and it made his hands clench. She said it as if she hadn't been lying to him. His chest ached harder. 'What are you doing here?' He tried to keep his voice even, but he knew his suspicions were about to be confirmed and that made evenness impossible. 'You told me you were spending the day at Poppy's.'

She gave a bored shrug and his hands clenched tighter. Where on earth had his madcap, full of laughter, full of fun daughter gone? When had she morphed into all this…*attitude*?

He didn't address the unknown woman who'd been talking to Stevie. He didn't even look at her. This was between him and his daughter. 'Well?' He tapped his foot—not that it helped to release much of the tension that had him coiled up tight. 'Well?' he demanded again.

Stevie tossed her head. Just for a moment something flickered behind her eyes—something he almost recognised—before her face became an ache of resentment. 'I've just signed on for the Miss Showgirl quest.'

Suspicion confirmed! He hauled in a breath. 'I told you I would not countenance you taking part in that contest.'

Countenance? When in his life had he ever used that word?

Stevie's eyes flashed. 'I decided not to take your advice.'

His control finally slipped. 'It wasn't advice. It was an order!' Stevie enter some stupid beauty pageant? Over his dead body!

He was in charge of his daughter's moral well-being. Letting her get involved in some shallow sham of a contest that objectified women and led young girls to believe their looks were more important than anything else? He snorted. He'd seen what that kind of obsession had done to Sonya. *Those* weren't the kind of values he wanted to instil in Stevie. Family, commitment, the long haul—those were things worth pursuing.

'You can haul your butt back in there and unregister yourself. *Now!* You are not taking part in that contest!'

'No.'

The single word chilled him. And it made him blink. Stevie had never openly defied him before.

'I'm sixteen.' She planted her hands on her hips. 'In another two years I'll be allowed to vote. I have a right to make some decisions about my life and I'm making this one. I'm entering Miss Showgirl whether you like it or not. Whether you support me or not.'

For a moment he could barely think. A part of him even acknowledged that she might have a point.

'And, regardless of what you think,' she suddenly yelled at him, 'Blair Macintyre thinks I have a chance!'

With that she turned and fled in the direction of home.

Blair Macintyre? The name flooded his mind, freezing him. *Blair Macintyre?* He wished to God that woman had never been born. Or at least that she'd been born and had grown up somewhere other than Dungog. For the life of him he couldn't remember her, but the constant refrain he'd heard during the course of his marriage to Sonya had been, *Blair Macintyre* this and *Blair Macintyre* that. Here she was on the cover of some glossy magazine. There she was on the catwalk in Paris…London…New York. Wherever!

If Blair Macintyre can do it then so can I!

And Sonya had. But that world had destroyed her. He would not let that happen to Stevie. He would do anything to protect his little girl.

The sound of a throat being cleared snapped him to. Damn it, he'd forgotten all about that unknown woman. He turned towards her. 'I'm Nicholas Conway, and I'm sorry you—'

Everything inside him clenched up tight when he finally came face to face with the woman. He swore once, hard. Then he laughed—only the laughter wasn't real laughter, it was bitterness. 'Blair Macintyre, right?'

He might not remember her, but Sonya had shoved enough pictures of Blair beneath his nose for him to recognise her. She was beautiful…gorgeous. Perfect. Magazine-cover perfect. And he knew it was a lie, because no real woman could look this good. She was the kind of woman who would fill a teenage girl's head with all sorts of unrealistic expectations about herself and her body. With her perfect pout and thick, lush lashes, her perfectly arched brows and her long blonde locks.

He was thirty-four. She had to be at least thirty-six. But she didn't look a day over twenty-five. More lies.

And yet, to his horror, his body responded to all that perfection. White-hot tendrils of desire licked along his veins, sparking nerve-endings with heat and hunger. Warmth flushed his skin. One knee twitched. His fingers literally ached to reach out and touch her cheek to see if her skin was as soft as it looked. What would she taste like? What would she feel like if he held her close? What would—?

He snapped off the images that bombarded him; thrust them out of his head. He was an experienced adult. If she could manipulate *him* like this, what kind of impact would she have on an impressionable sixteen-year-old?

Her lips suddenly twisted. 'Let me guess. I don't look any different, right?'

The words drawled out of her, their husky notes caressing his skin. She raised one of those perfectly shaped eyebrows and his body reacted with heat, his tongue reacted with anger. 'What the hell are you talking about?'

For some inconceivable reason she seemed to brighten at that.

It disappeared a moment later when he leant towards her and snapped, 'Stay away from my daughter.'

CHAPTER TWO

THE woman had eyes so blue they could steal a man's soul, and as Nick stared into them they made him ache for something he couldn't name. She pursed those delectable lips and it suddenly hit him how loud, coarse, and utterly unreasonable he must seem to her.

That would be because he was *acting* loud, coarse, and utterly unreasonable. *Get a grip!* He pinched the bridge of his nose between thumb and forefinger, backed up a step so that he was no longer crowding her. Once upon a time he'd have approached a situation like this with charm and humour, doing his best to deflect and defuse any bad feelings.

Once upon a time…

When had the world turned upside down?

When Stevie had started spending all her pocket money on make-up and fashion magazines, spending too much of her time window-shopping for clothes, that was when. She was talking about getting her ears pierced. *Pierced!* She wanted to maim her body in the interests of fashion? As far as he was concerned that made no sense whatsoever.

And it reminded him too much of Sonya.

Blair drew herself up to her full height. He was six feet two. She must be five feet eleven. Sonya had been the same height.

Stop it. This woman wasn't Sonya. She hadn't abandoned and then almost bankrupted her family. She hadn't succumbed to designer drugs. Even if she did represent the world of fashion that he loathed—the same world that had destroyed Sonya—that didn't mean she deserved his rudeness or to bear the brunt of his frustration.

He opened his mouth to form some sort of apology, to try and explain why he was yelling at her like a lunatic. But not only had she straightened, she'd folded her arms—and it thrust her breasts out, pressed them tight against her T-shirt. The heat and the hunger hit him again. The words dried in his mouth.

He forced his gaze back to hers to find her surveying him. Sympathy gleamed from those mesmerising eyes. 'You're the faithless father?' She gave a tiny shake of her head.

It took a moment for her words to hit him. *The what?*

'Mr Conway, I know this is none of my business, but… But I think you'll find that your daughter has misinterpreted your lack of support for the Miss Showgirl as a belief that she's not good enough to enter.'

He stiffened.

'Sixteen-year-old girls can be terribly vulnerable and their confidence shaky. While I don't doubt for a moment that it hasn't been your intention to sabotage her self-confidence, that's the effect it has had.'

Sabotaging Stevie? Garbage! He was protecting her. Any sense of proportion he'd gained shot off into the ether with the speed of a V8 super car. 'Don't you tell me how to raise my daughter!'

She blinked. 'I'm not. I'm just saying—'

'Well, don't bother!' His hand slashed the space between them. 'What the hell do you know about teenage girls?'

She tilted her chin. 'I *was* one.'

'Do you have children?'

He watched her swallow. His knee twitched again. 'No.'

'Then don't presume to tell me how to deal with

my own. If I don't think it's appropriate for her to enter a beauty contest—'

'It's not just a beauty contest!' Colour flared in her cheeks. 'It's for charity, and it's a chance for the girls—'

'Save the spiel! I don't want Stevie involved in some sad, jumped-up little beauty pageant and I want you to stay away from her. You hear me?'

'Me *and* the neighbours, I should think.'

He grimaced. He was going to have to apologise. The thought did not improve his temper. He started to compose a suitable apology. He opened his mouth to deliver it—

'You do know that Stevie believes you don't think she's pretty, don't you?'

Air left his lungs. Stevie was beautiful, unique. She was the light of his life. She had to know that. Not pretty? Stevie could win the Miss Showgirl quest hands down. She was the prettiest, smartest—

He cut the thought off, annoyed with himself for even going there. He needed to talk to Stevie as soon as he could. He straightened. 'I don't believe we have anything else to discuss.'

Her eyes widened. She even had the gall to roll them.

'Darn city slicker,' he muttered under his breath, needing to vent.

'Country hick,' she shot back, and he almost choked. *She'd heard him?*

With a lift of one elegant shoulder she turned and sauntered off. He stared after her until she'd disappeared around the corner.

He dragged a hand down his face and bit back a curse. He'd been darn rude. He'd let his temper and frustration get the better of him, and that hadn't happened in a long, *long* time. What had got into him?

He swung away and kicked at a stone before striding back to the car. He didn't know what he was going to do about Stevie and this Miss Showgirl nonsense, but one thing he did know—he was going to have to apologise to Blair Macintyre.

'You did what?'

Nick swallowed at Stevie's screech. He'd never heard her take that tone before. Her voice literally bounced off the kitchen walls. He forced his shoulders back. 'I told you I didn't want you involved in anything as shallow and superficial as a beauty contest. You should be focussing on your studies. If you want to be lawyer then you'll need good grades.'

Stevie dragged her hands back through her hair. 'This is about Mum, isn't it?'

He ran a finger around the collar of his T-shirt. 'This is about you.'

'Because I want to look nice, you think that makes me like Mum. You think I'm going to use drugs!'

'That's absurd.' He'd done his best to shield Stevie from the truth about her mother's death, but Sonya's overdose had made all the national newspapers.

She stepped back, her face going pale. 'You don't trust me.'

Tears shimmered in her eyes. Her pain cut him to the quick. 'I want you to focus on important things, not shallow nonsense.' He would *not* lose another girl he loved to the ruthless, heartless world of fashion. He would *not* let Stevie starve herself, turn to surgery, and turn herself inside out all in the name of presenting some impossible ideal vision for the camera.

'The Miss Showgirl quest isn't just a beauty contest.' Her voice wobbled. She paced around the kitchen table. An image of Blair flashed in his mind. 'It was my one chance, and you've wrecked it!'

He stiffened. 'Your one chance at what?'

'To learn how to dress well! To learn how to do my hair and make-up, and—'

'There's nothing wrong with how you look!'

'Yes, there is!' The words burst from her in frustration, her face red and her hands shaking. 'You're a guy—what do you know? You want all the other lawyers laughing at me the way the girls at school do?'

Country hick. Blair's taunt ran through his mind.

'The other girls have their mothers. I…'

He stared at her. He'd never felt more at a loss.

'Even if Miss Showgirl is as superficial as you say, what's wrong with wanting to play around with make-up and hair and wearing pretty things? I'm tired of pretending not to like those things because you don't approve.' Her voice rose again. 'I don't care what you say. That doesn't make me like Mum!'

'I wasn't saying—' He broke off because that was exactly what he'd been saying. All those things—pretty clothes, make-up, fussing with hair—they reminded him of what Sonya had chosen over her family. Over him. And, worst of all, what she had chosen over Stevie.

His eyes started to burn and his temples throbbed. Stevie had forgone all those things—things girls delighted in—to spare his feelings?

She leant across the table towards him, her face distorted with frustration and disappointment. 'It was my one chance to get over being afraid.'

'What are you afraid of?' He'd slay any dragon for her.

'Public speaking!' she all but hollered at him. 'It's part of Miss Showgirl to make a speech. We get lessons, pointers. But now... How will I ever be a lawyer if I can't speak in public?'

The breath shot out of him. He should have talked to her, found out why the quest meant so much to her. Instead he'd jumped to conclusions, and then he'd jumped in to play the heavy.

She was right. He hadn't trusted her.

'Baby, I—'

But she wouldn't let him speak. 'You don't think I can win.'

Her voice was hard, but there was a wobble beneath it that snagged at his heart.

'You think I'll make a fool of myself like everyone else does.'

His hands clenched. Everyone who?

'But Blair thought I had a chance. Blair believed in me.'

With that, she raced out of the room. Her bedroom door slammed and then he heard muffled sobs. He closed his eyes, pressed a fist to his brow. Stevie rarely cried.

It took all his strength to remain in his seat and not go to her. She wouldn't welcome his attempts at comfort at the moment. He'd made such a hash of this.

He had to fix it.

He rose. He picked up his hat and dusted if off against his thigh. He knew Blair was Glory Middleton's niece. If she was staying in Dungog, that was where she'd be. He settled the hat on his head and made for the front door.

A tap on the back door had Blair glancing up from her magazine. She'd not long got home and her pulse had barely slowed from her encounter with Nicholas Conway.

What a Neanderthal!

A sexy Neanderthal, though.

The thought slithered in beneath her guard. She shook it off and pushed to her feet to answer the door, almost welcoming the promised distraction on the other side. She was off men for good. And a Neanderthal was still a Neanderthal—sexy or otherwise.

She opened the door, and then pulled up short when she saw who stood on the other side of the screen.

And just like that her pulse sped up again.

An adrenaline surge as her body readied itself for another confrontation, she rationalised. She opened the screen door, folded her arms, and leant a shoulder against the doorframe. She didn't invite him in. She knew how to do cool and haughty. And at the moment, cool and haughty pleased her nicely. 'Well, well, if it isn't the country…boy.'

She couldn't call him a hick again because a) she wasn't angry any more, and b) he quite obviously wasn't a hick.

Her mouth went dry. He was *hot*!

He wore faded denim jeans and a black T-shirt that hugged his shoulders, emphasising their breadth. Her gaze drifted over those shoulders and slowly made their way down his body. The thin black cotton emphasised the muscles in his chest before plastering itself to an abdomen that even through the material she could see was sculpted and lean. Her pulse sped up even more. Lean hips. Long legs. Feet encased in dusty brown work-boots. This country boy had country chic down pat, but he was sexier than any male model she'd come across.

She suspected he wasn't trying to sport any look at all. She had a feeling that what you saw with Nicholas Conway was exactly what you got.

It was beyond sexy.

She tossed her hair—her wig. Not that she was interested in sexy or sex. She couldn't imagine being intimate with a man ever again. The thought of a man seeing her naked body…

She suppressed a shudder. She could imagine with a vividness that made her stomach rebel a man recoiling in horror when he saw the real her—scars and all. Could imagine being rejected. Again.

So she lifted her chin and kept her demeanour cold and haughty. 'Something you forgot to hol-ler?' she drawled.

He scratched a hand through his hair. He shuf-fled his feet. He held his hat in his hands and restless fingers twirled it round and round. Her stomach softened.

Neanderthal—don't forget that.

'I wanted to apologise.'

She could tell by the way he held himself that he was waiting for her to slam the door in his face. She'd never been one for grand, melodramatic gestures. Still, the idea was tempting. His eyes flashed and glittered as he waited for her response. With a sigh, she relented. 'I suppose you'd better come in.'

She could feel his bulk behind her as he followed her into the kitchen, his vital heat. There was something purely masculine about it. She put the kitchen table between them. 'Coffee? Tea? Something stronger?' He didn't look like the kind of man who needed Dutch courage, although with her last boyfriend she'd proved that where men were concerned she had seriously bad judgement. Who knew what Nick was really like?

'Are you having anything?'

He'd donned his best manners. She had to give him that. 'I was about to make tea.'

'Tea would be great. If you're sure it isn't any trouble.'

Yep, his very best manners. And just like that

she didn't want him to apologise any more. She wanted him and his disturbing presence and her even more disturbing reaction to him to walk out through that door and leave her in peace.

For a brief moment today she'd experienced something she hadn't felt in quite some time—optimism. She'd felt she had something of value to offer to someone. Namely Stevie. And then this man had come along and deflated it with his harsh words and dismissive attitude.

Still, it had been refreshing to be abused rather than mollycoddled.

She snapped herself back into the present and put the jug on to boil, spooned tea into the pot. Nicholas and his unnerving masculinity weren't going to walk out through that door just yet, because she'd offered him tea as hospitality demanded. The sooner the tea was done, the sooner he'd leave.

She chose her aunt's tiniest teacups instead of her usual generous mugs.

He didn't speak until they were seated at the kitchen table and Blair had poured the tea.

He didn't speak even then. She bit back a sigh. 'You said you wanted to apologise?'

He nodded, surveying her over the rim of his

cup, his eyes not wavering from hers. 'That's right.'

She bit back another sigh. It came from deep down inside her, wistful and full of yearning for something she didn't want to look at too closely. 'Apology accepted. Forget about it.' Life was too short to hold grudges.

'Hey, I haven't made it yet. Besides, it's not that simple, city girl.' He smiled, but there were shadows in his eyes. 'Earlier, you said something about looking exactly the same. What did you mean?'

'Nothing. Forget about it.' Their gazes clashed and locked, and she cursed her rotten defensive self-consciousness. Earlier he'd looked at her as if he'd liked what he saw—really liked it—and for a moment something inside her had responded.

And then she'd remembered the scars, no right breast, no hair—and had imagined his reaction if he could see the real her. Those tart words had come spilling out of her mouth before she could stop them.

His eyes refused to release her. 'I've been ill.' She was the first to break eye contact. 'But I'm all better again.'

Better? Yes.

Would a man ever find her attractive again? Unlikely.

He didn't say anything for a long moment. She risked a glance at him. He shook his head. 'I'm sorry you've been ill, Blair. You're home to recuperate?'

'I'm recuperated.' She wanted to be clear about that. 'I'm home for some R&R. A holiday.'

His eyes narrowed. She refused to let hers drop this time. Finally he shook his head. 'None of that changes the fact that I shouldn't have lost my temper and said the things I did without a thought for anything but my…'

'Your?' She preferred to follow his train of thought than her own.

He set his teacup down. 'Fear.'

It shouldn't be sexy when a man admitted to being afraid. Only, where Nicholas Conway was concerned, it was. Maybe it was the way he held her gaze as he made the admission. She moistened suddenly dry lips. He watched the action and his eyes darkened. It was hellishly sexy.

Hellish.

'Fear never brings out the best in a man, and it seems I was hellbent on yelling at someone.'

She saw now that maybe he'd needed to.

He grimaced. 'If I'd known you'd been sick, though…'

'No harm done on my account. Like I said, I'm well again now.' She nearly spread her arms to add, *Don't I look the picture of health*? Only on further consideration she didn't want him looking at her that closely. He might take it as an invitation, as flirting.

She wasn't inviting anything.

'Blair, I really am very sorry. My behaviour was appalling.'

'Apology accepted.' *Please go now.*

'The thing is, I've screwed up royally and I need to make amends.'

'Not to me.'

'A bit to you,' he said cautiously, 'and a lot to Stevie.'

She sat back.

'Which is why I need you to forgive me.'

'Because…?'

'Because I'm taking back everything I said, I'm asking that Stevie be reinstated as an entrant for the Miss Showgirl quest, and I'm begging you to help Stevie the way you told her you would.'

He took a sip of his tea, as if his throat needed the moisture after that admission. His big hand on the tiny teacup should have looked clumsy, but it didn't. His eyes surveyed her over the rim and she remembered all the things he'd said about the Miss Showgirl quest. He'd implied that it was a waste of time, a waste of brains, and a waste of talent, and by association that she was worthless too.

And yet with one look he could have her prickling and burning all over. He'd come here fully expecting to be forgiven, presuming she'd be happy to bend over backwards to help him out.

And she had. And she was. And that made her angry too.

'And what happens next week when you change your mind all over again? Will I find you banging on my door to hurl more abuse at me?'

His jaw dropped. 'Of course not.'

'You expect me to take your word for that? I don't know you from Adam.'

'I—'

'Have you changed your mind about the…?' She cocked her head to one side. 'What was it? Sad, jumped-up little beauty pageant?'

He didn't say anything and she realised he hadn't changed his mind about anything. But he was still going to let Stevie enter? She folded her arms, intrigued despite her best intentions.

'If I hadn't interfered, if I hadn't lost my cool, you'd still be happy to help Stevie out like you'd told her you would.'

She had every intention of keeping her promise to Stevie. Still, it wouldn't hurt him to sweat for a bit. 'But now I have to take into account a temperamental parent.'

He half rose out of his chair. 'I'm *not* temperamental!'

'Are you yelling at me, Mr Conway?'

He subsided back into his seat. 'No,' he muttered. 'It's just...Stevie shouldn't pay for my mistake.'

No, she shouldn't.

'And it's Nicholas—Nick—not Mr Conway.'

Blair considered him for a moment. She almost chuckled at the way he tried to hide his glower. 'I was right, wasn't I? Stevie took your lack of support to mean you didn't believe she had a scarecrow's chance of winning. I'm right, aren't I?'

His deepening scowl told her she was.

'You're enjoying this, aren't you?' he ground out.

'I am taking a fiendish kind of delight in it.' She didn't scruple to admit it.

'And when will you deem that I've been punished enough?'

'Oh, your punishment hasn't even begun yet, Mr—'

'Nick!' he snapped. His hand clenched to a fist on the table. 'Will you help Stevie?' he burst out. 'Please?'

He loved his daughter. He wanted her to be happy. And he hated the Miss Showgirl quest.

'I will help Stevie on one condition, Nicholas. That you support her fully in her Miss Showgirl efforts.'

'Sure I will. I'm here, aren't I?'

Her smile grew, and she continued as if he hadn't spoken. 'By taking on the role of her fundraising manager. By co-ordinating and directing all her fundraising efforts.'

Nick's jaw dropped. 'You can't expect me to...' He let the sentence trail off. The pictures rising in his mind were too hideous to put into words. Him get involved in the dog-eat-dog world of a beauty pageant?

She sent him a pitying glance. 'Oh, no, Nicholas. I expect a whole lot more than that.'

His stomach clenched to hard ball of lead. 'More?' he croaked.

'But fundraising manager will do for a start.'

He wouldn't know where to begin.

'You were serious weren't you? About making it up to Stevie?'

'Yes, but…'

'Words are cheap.'

He saw then that she was right. He could repeat over and over again until he was blue in the face that he had faith in her, he could say it till the cows came home—and he would the moment he got home—but the only way to truly reassure Stevie, to prove that he believed in her, was to support her in a material way. Like co-ordinating her fundraising efforts.

On the up side, being involved did mean he'd have a chance of protecting her against the more unsavoury aspects of the pageant, the competitiveness and bitchiness and constant undermining of one's self-esteem…

'It looks as though you have yourself a deal, city girl.' He could have sworn, though, that when he extended his hand she was curiously reluctant to take it.

Blair might act all haughty and aloof, but somehow he knew he'd needled his way in under her skin. The thought made him grin. It made him hold her hand for longer than custom demanded.

When he finally released her the colour in her cheeks was high and a purely masculine satisfaction settled in the pit of his stomach.

Game on.

CHAPTER THREE

THE moment Nick realised where his thoughts were headed he snatched them back. He wasn't messing about with a woman like Blair Macintyre. He'd allowed one woman to dash all his dreams. He wasn't giving another one that same opportunity.

He'd achieved what he'd set out to—he'd apologised to Blair and made sure she'd still help Stevie. He'd done what he could to put things back to the way they'd been before he'd so stupidly interfered.

Yet he found himself curiously reluctant to end this meeting, thank Blair, and leave. The colour in her cheeks had receded. He wanted to see—to *make*—that colour high again.

Her teacup clattered to her saucer as if the way he studied her unnerved her.

Because he wasn't just studying her—he was staring!

He forced his gaze down to the table and drained what was left in his tiny teacup. Glory would have given him tea in a mug, but Blair had sophisticated city ways. She had gloss and elegance. Would she offer him another cup?

'So Stevie really socked it to you, huh?'

'She cried.' Bile churned in his throat. 'And she hardly ever cries.'

He risked a glance at her—*no staring*—and found her delectable lips pursed and her eyes soft with sympathy. He memorised every curve of those lips before lifting his eyes. Their gazes locked and held. His heart slowed and then surged against his ribs.

Blair shot to her feet as if in sudden panic, as if to race away.

He sat back, blinked, and did his best to dislodge his heart from his throat. And then her panic, if that was what it had been, was wiped away and replaced with a thrust out chin and hands planted on slender hips. He wondered if he'd imagined the panic.

He didn't think so.

He stared at the determined picture she made now and found his muscles bunching. He couldn't make head nor tail of this woman.

'Well, what are we waiting for?'

He rose to his feet at her regal tone. 'Waiting for?' he ventured.

'Don't you want to make things right again for Stevie as soon as you can?'

Sure he did, but… 'Stevie won't talk to me until at least dinnertime.' Which was hours away yet.

'Which serves you right. But I expect she'll talk to me.'

His shoulders unhitched. 'You'll talk to her?'

Her lips twisted as if she was trying to hold back a smile. 'Of course I will.'

'I…' He couldn't think of a darn thing to say to that, so he followed her out through the door and waited while she locked it.

'*You* deserve to stew for a while yet, country boy, but Stevie doesn't.'

'I could kiss you,' he said fervently.

She took a step away from him. 'I'd rather you didn't.'

She could do ice queen as if it was second nature. She grinned suddenly and ice queen transformed to temptress. His blood, and other parts of him, heated up. She rubbed her hands together before motioning to him to lead the way.

Glory's house was only two streets away from where his automotive workshop fronted the town's

main street. The weatherboard cottage he called
home was out at the back.

'Everyone in town is going to know about your
turnaround in relation to the Miss Showgirl quest
now. It's going to be beautiful to watch.'

Her relish had his mouth kicking upwards. 'Not
going to work.'

She widened her eyes, mock innocent. 'Work?'

'You're not going to get a rise out of me that
easily, princess.'

'Peasant.'

Energy fired through him. He found it suddenly
easy to laugh. Then he frowned. When had it become hard to laugh?

'So tell me...'

He shook the sombre reflection aside and readied himself for her next thrust.

'What approach are you going to take with the
fundraising?'

As far as thrusts went it wasn't bad. 'Any ideas?'

'Oodles—and for every three you come up with
I'll give you one.'

He tried to look injured. 'That hardly seems
fair.'

'It's called penance.'

He threw his head back and let loose with another laugh. 'Why don't you really stick the knife in? I'm sure there's a spot here somewhere…' he pointed to his chest '…that you've missed.'

She grinned back, and it occurred to him that she was enjoying their exchange as much as he was.

He ushered her though the back entrance of the repair shop, opening the tall gate for her. He watched her take in the large galvanised-iron shed to the left and the neat weatherboard house opposite. The space between was hard-packed earth. There was an outdoor table setting against the far wall. No garden. He couldn't tell what she was thinking.

It unsettled him to find he cared what she thought. Light—he had to keep it light. 'Slave-driver,' he muttered.

She tossed that long blonde hair of hers. 'Grease monkey.'

Her good-natured insult released his tension and another laugh.

'You're a mechanic, huh?'

'Yep.'

'My car needs a service.'

He wasn't a run-of-the-mill mechanic. He restored classic cars. He had a national reputation for it. These days he could pick and choose what projects he wanted to work on.

None of that stopped him from saying, 'Bring it in on Thursday or Friday.'

'Thank you.'

'No.' He touched her arm before she could set off towards the house. 'Thank *you* for coming here to see Stevie, and for showing me how to make it up to her. I still don't approve of this preoccupation with looks and fashion, but I do appreciate you coming here.'

She took a step away from him, out of his reach so his hand dropped back to his side. She hitched her chin in just *that* way. 'Stevie and I will prove to you how wrong you are.'

'It doesn't matter if I'm wrong or right. I need to show Stevie that I trust her enough to support the decisions she makes even if I don't like them. I ranted at you like an angry bull and you've had the grace to overlook it, as well as the generosity to agree to help Stevie. I'm in your debt, city girl.'

Her eyes suddenly narrowed. 'I'll be paying for my car service, Nicholas. I wasn't after a freebie.'

And, because his gratitude had obviously embarrassed her, he made himself laugh and say, 'I'll be charging you top dollar.'

Blair didn't smile back. 'Just because I used to be a model, you've written me off as shallow, frivolous, and incapable of depth, gravity or any kind of finer feeling, haven't you?'

'I…' He rolled his shoulders. It struck him that that was exactly what he'd done. He'd tarred Blair with the same brush as Sonya. On what grounds? After all, what did he really know about Blair Macintyre?

Zilch.

Except that she'd forgiven his bad behaviour. And that she was kind enough to want to help Stevie.

And neither of those things indicated shallowness or a lack of finer feeling. 'Blair, I—'

She stabbed a finger at him. 'What would your reaction be, I wonder, if I told you I'd spent a considerable time in front of the mirror this morning putting on my make-up?'

'What's a considerable amount of time?' he ground out. 'More than half an hour?' Were these the things that she was going to teach his daughter were important?

'Oh, yes.'

'Why the hell is that necessary?'

'And what would you say if I told you I was wearing false eyelashes?'

No!

'And what would you think if I told you I was wearing a wig?'

He took a step back. 'The hell you are.' He found himself shaking as he moved forward again to push his face in close to hers. '*Are* you wearing a wig, Blair?'

'I am,' she shot back at him, her eyes blazing as she tossed her head. All that glorious fake hair swished round her shoulders and down her back, taunting him with the lie it represented. 'What I want to know is, why does it matter?'

He unclenched his jaw to say, 'You can even *ask* me that? You represent everything I hate about the world of fashion.' Couldn't she see the damage she and people like her did to mere mortals— *to teenage girls*? 'You want to fill my daughter's head with a load of unrealistic expectations. She's going to feel compelled to live up to those expectations and—'

'You should have more faith in your daughter.' She shot right back again. 'There's absolutely nothing wrong with a woman wanting to look the best she can.'

'Except when it takes over her life.' *A wig?* 'Like it's obviously taken over yours! Take the damn wig off, Blair. Let my daughter see you as you really are rather than filling her head with a load of fantastic lies.'

Just for a moment he could have sworn that hurt flashed through her eyes. 'So you think it's all about vanity, huh?'

He didn't say anything.

'Are you giving me an ultimatum—take off my wig or you won't let me see Stevie?'

He steeled himself against that hurt. 'That's right.'

'When *I'm* doing *you* a favour by coming here?'

'Filling Stevie's head with nonsense isn't doing me *or* her a favour.'

'If I don't take my wig off are you *still* going to forbid her to enter Miss Showgirl?'

He shuffled his feet. No, he couldn't do that. It meant too much to Stevie. But he didn't have to admit as much to Blair. Not yet.

Her eyes suddenly flashed their scorn, blasting the skin on his face and arms. She had no right to direct that at him. All he was trying to do was protect his daughter from being beguiled by false images.

'Oh, for heaven's sake, Nicholas,' she snapped. 'Put two and two together.'

He opened his mouth. He closed it again. The soft vulnerability of her mouth belied the hard jut of her chin. Her nostrils flared and her shoulders had gone rigid. And her voice… It didn't sound like her voice.

A chill edged up his spine.

She stuck out a hip, her assumed nonchalance at odds with the expression in her eyes. *'Let me guess. I look exactly the same, right?'* She mimicked her own earlier words.

He swallowed.

She rolled her eyes, but the darkness in them contradicted her implied impatience. *'I've been ill.'*

She cocked an eyebrow, as if daring him to join the dots, to put the pieces of the puzzle together, to make the connection between her wig and having been sick.

And he did.

He gripped a fencepost to keep himself upright as the breath rushed out of his body. Her gaze shied away from his then, as if she couldn't bear to see what was reflected in his eyes. 'Why did you automatically assume the make-up and the wig were for the purposes of vanity, huh? Do you always jump to such appalling conclusions?'

He hated himself in that moment for the prejudice that had blinded him.

'I'm not wearing a wig to hide a bad haircut or a disastrous dye-job. I wish!' She gave a laugh— only it wasn't a laugh. It was a sound masquerading as a laugh and it sliced through him like a physical pain. 'I don't have enough hair to either cut *or* dye!'

He closed his eyes, hating himself even more for the reprehensible judgements he'd made, for the accusations he'd flung at her.

'Chemotherapy,' she said, as if now that she'd started she couldn't stop.

'Cancer?' he croaked.

'Cancer,' she affirmed.

He pushed away from the fence. He wanted to offer her comfort, to say he was sorry, to wrap her in his arms and assure himself she was all right. He didn't. She'd probably sock him one. And he'd deserve it.

'It's hell on hair.' She pointed to her lashes and eyebrows. 'The good news is that I won't have to wax my legs for a while.'

The shadows in her eyes would haunt him for ever. 'Blair, I'm—'

'Do you know what I look like without all this hair and make-up?'

'I—'

'With round cheeks and a big, bald, round head?'

Her eyes flashed their fury. She planted her hands on her hips, evidently awaiting an answer. *She'd still look beautiful.* As soon as the thought filtered into his consciousness he realised he meant it. It struck him then with equal force that she wouldn't believe him.

'I look like a great big helpless baby, that's what. And you know how people treat a baby, don't you?'

Her fury, her frustration, had started to run out of steam. She all but limped over to a low brick wall and sat. She dragged in a breath that made her whole frame shudder.

'Like they can't do even the simplest things for themselves,' she finished on a whisper.

It was the way her shoulders slumped that cut him to the quick. He collapsed down on the wall beside her. He rested his elbows on his knees, dropped his head to his hands. How did he apologise after what he'd just done, said, the accusations he'd hurled at her?

'You can mock and scorn my wig and my false eyelashes and my false eyebrows all you want, Mr Conway. You can tell me I'm a liar, that I'm vain, that the image I present is a sham. You can tell me I have my priorities all wrong. But know this…'

Another breath made her entire body shudder. He wanted to hand her a big stick and ask her to beat him with it. That might make him feel better, but he suspected it would only make her feel worse. He'd misjudged her in every conceivable way. Why? Because once upon a time she'd been a model. On that evidence he'd decided she was shallow.

Nausea threatened to choke him.

She met his gaze and her blue-eyed anguish flayed him more effectively than any big stick ever could.

'The way I present myself is my defence against the world. It is my attempt to regain a portion of control over my life.' Her eyes told him she'd been to hell and back. 'It is my way of trying to get my life back to normal. That means people treating me the way they did before I got sick. The only way I can make that happen is to look as normal as I can—to look the way I used to before…'

She hiccupped. His heart slumped to his knees, but he forced himself to straighten. 'Are you sure you're well enough to be getting back to normal?'

'Oh!' Her lip curled. 'Not that you've just proved my point or anything! Did that thought occur to you when you were abusing me earlier?'

'No, but…' A person could pull off a hell of a show with hair and make-up.

'You didn't think I was weak and feeble then. And I bet all the tea in China that you wouldn't have yelled at me if hadn't been wearing my wig!'

The Chinese tea was all hers. But… 'You *want* to be yelled at?'

'I want to be treated like normal. The way I really look makes people treat me like I'm an invalid and that makes me feel like a freak.'

He'd made her feel like a freak.

'And I'm tired of pity.' Her eyes narrowed. 'I want my life back.'

He admired her quiet dignity. He admired her courage.

He hated himself.

'Blair, I shouldn't have made the assumptions

I did. I shouldn't have said what I did. I'm sorry.
I wish—'

He wished he could take back all those things
he'd said. He wished he could turn the clock back.
He wished he could wave a magic wand so that
she'd never been sick.

She straightened. 'I want to be judged for myself, not by my illness. And not because I used to
be a model once upon a time.'

One thing he would never do again was judge
someone on their looks, or the fact that they were
or had been a model. But before he could tell her
that, she rose. So formal. All their former teasing
and banter, the digs and challenges, the traded in-
sults were a distant memory. That suddenly felt
like such a loss.

'Tell Stevie I'll look forward to seeing her on
Thursday evening.'

She wanted to be away from him as soon as she
could. And he had no one to blame but himself.

Blair forced one foot in front of the other. She
ordered herself not to look back to see if Nick
watched her.

The prickling and burning at the back of her
neck told her he did.

The look on his face when—

Well done, you idiot! Revealing the reason she wore a wig had been supposed to teach him a lesson. Teach him to not jump to conclusions. But…

What had she been thinking? Now all Nick would see whenever he looked at her was her illness.

She tried to banish his look of horror from her mind. She counted her footsteps instead, all the way around the corner and halfway down the next street, where she promptly forgot what number she was up to. She halted and went to grind her palms against her eyes—before remembering her false eyelashes and all her carefully applied eye make-up. She gripped her hands in front of her.

The look on his face!

Horror, that was what he'd felt, and it had reminded her of Adam's horror. The thought of her appearance had horrified Adam. Appalled Adam. Repelled Adam.

She forced her feet forward, swallowed the lump in her throat, and lifted her chin. Well, Nick Conway didn't have to worry, because she'd make sure that from now on they'd barely clap eyes on each other.

She did her best to put him out of her mind

as she stomped the rest of the way home. It was pointless regretting what she looked like. It was pointless caring what someone like Nick thought of her. For heaven's sake, she'd survived breast cancer. She should be grateful and count her blessings.

She let herself in at the back door and was immediately greeted with the scent of toasted cheese sandwiches. On cue her mouth watered, the scent transporting her back in time to when she'd been a schoolgirl.

Glory glanced around from the toaster oven and pressed a hand to her heart. 'I was starting to get worried. I didn't know where you'd disappeared to. Which is why—' She gestured to the toasting sandwiches. 'The scent of these always had you emerging from the woodwork.' Her smile didn't hide her concern.

Blair's heart dipped. 'I was just out and about. You shouldn't worry about me so much, Aunt Glory. I'm fine.'

'Yes, dear.' But it was an automatic response, not a proclamation of faith in Blair's recovering health. 'Have you been up to anything fun?'

She was about to reply in the negative but curiosity niggled at her. She gave in to it. 'I had a couple of…odd encounters with Nicholas Conway.'

'Nick?' Glory's eyebrows lifted. 'He's a nice-looking boy.'

She remembered the exchanges she and her aunt had shared when she'd been a teenager. She bit back a grin and gave an exaggerated snort. 'Nice-looking? Oh, Aunt Glory, you can do better than that. The man is hot!'

Glory's eyes almost started from her head, and then they started to dance. 'Super-hunk?'

'Better,' Blair allowed. 'But this hot super-hunk of ours has ordered me to stay away from his daughter.'

'Stevie?'

She nodded. 'He had a real bee in his bonnet about the Miss Showgirl quest. What's the goss there?'

Glory shook her head. 'Nick keeps to himself.' She dished out the sandwiches and then frowned. 'Though strictly speaking that's not exactly true. He coaches the under-sixteen cricket team in the summer, and the under-ten soccer team in winter, and has lots of work-experience kids through his workshop.'

She handed Blair a plate and took a seat at the

table. Blair took the seat opposite—the seat Nick had sat in earlier—pulled a corner off her sandwich, and popped it in her mouth. 'And?'

'He married young, but it ended badly and they separated. And then Stevie's mother died. It was all very tragic. To the best of my knowledge there hasn't been anyone serious in Nick's life since.'

Blair reddened under her aunt's suddenly alert gaze. 'None of my business.' She seized her sandwich and bit into it. 'But that's a terribly sad story.' Poor Nick and Stevie. And that poor young woman. Blair's own brush with mortality was still too fresh for her to not acknowledge that.

'Well, it's quite a while ago now. Must be over twelve years.'

They ate in silence for a while.

'Nick's done well for himself, though,' Glory finally said. 'He's become quite a business force in the town. Eight years ago he bought the service station next to that workshop of his, and then five years ago he bought a heavy-machinery leasing business. He practically owns all of the real estate on the block that he lives on, and he must employ close to ten people. Rumour has it that he means to expand the leasing business—there's a real demand from the mines, apparently—which will create even more jobs.'

He'd managed all that while raising a daughter on his own? Blair found herself developing a new respect for Nick Conway.

'So Stevie is going to withdraw from the quest?'

For the first time since she'd walked away from Nick earlier she grinned—really grinned. Because, regardless of whatever other battles she'd lost today, she'd won that one. 'Oh, no.'

Glory leant forward, as if in anticipation of whatever her niece was about to say, and it suddenly felt like old times. Glory's eyes danced, the lines around her mouth softened, and Blair treasured the moment. It gave her hope that things could eventually return to normal.

'Spill,' Glory ordered.

'Let's just say he saw the error of his ways and has now agreed to spearhead Stevie's fundraising campaign.'

Glory sat back and stared at her niece in admiration. 'Well done, you.'

She pretended to preen, but only for a moment. 'It was more Stevie's doing than mine. He'd do anything to make her happy.'

'Good-looking *and* good-hearted.'

'And let's not forget successful and well-off.'

Glory laughed, as Blair had meant her to. As far as she was concerned, though, Nick Conway was history.

On Thursday Blair took her car to Nick's garage for a service, because a) her car needed to be serviced, and b) Nick's might not be the only automotive workshop in town, but he'd find out if she took her car to somebody else for servicing. Dungog was that kind of town. And then he would know that their last encounter had mattered to her.

She didn't want him thinking that.

Even if she hadn't been able to stop replaying the soul-sickening moment when he'd croaked the word 'Cancer?' Or the horror that had filled his eyes when he'd realised that beneath her wig she was bald.

She grimaced again now, just thinking about it. At the exact same moment Nick emerged from beneath a car. Not just any car either, but a sleek and shiny XJ Jaguar.

He froze.

She did her best to stop grimacing.

'Hello.'

He didn't call her city girl.

'Hello.'

She didn't call him country boy.

She pointed behind her. 'There was no one in Reception.'

'My receptionist is sick today.'

'I, uh...' She swallowed and started again. 'You told me to bring my car in today or tomorrow. I hope that's still okay?' She bit her lip and mentally kicked herself. 'I probably should've rung and made a proper appointment.'

'No, no.' He scrambled to his feet and wiped his hands on a rag. 'I can fit you in.'

He's a nice-looking boy.

Man, Glory, she silently amended. He's a nice-looking *man*. Even in grease-splattered overalls.

He took the keys from her outstretched fingers. 'How are you feeling?'

Her lips twisted. *How are you feeling?* Not, *How are you?* or, *How has your day been?* or, *What have you been up to?* but *How are you feeling?*

She thrust out her chin and glared. 'I'm feeling fantastic!'

He eyed her warily.

She folded her arms. 'How are *you* feeling?'

He swallowed and then sent her a rueful grin.

'Like an idiot. Sorry, Blair, that came out all wrong.'

Because all he could see now was her illness. She kept her mouth shut. There wasn't anything to say. Her pulse had plenty to say about that cute grin, though.

'I like what you've done with your…hair.'

She'd had the wig cut short. The expression on Nick's face when he'd thought she wore a wig purely for vanity's sake had rubbed and chafed at her. Because, if she were honest, vanity *was* partly the reason, wasn't it? In disgust at herself, she'd asked her friend Dana to cut the wig to a more manageable length.

Dana had cut it an inch above Blair's shoulders and had added soft layers around her face. Blair lifted her chin. 'So do I.'

For one pulse-racing moment she thought he meant to reach out and touch it. She stepped back, her heart pounding hard. 'When will my car be ready?'

'Tomorrow afternoon, okay?'

She nodded, and then turned on her heel and fled—because it suddenly occurred to her that Nick's opinion had started to matter just a little too much.

CHAPTER FOUR

BLAIR hesitated at the office door of Nick's workshop late on Friday afternoon. This morning he'd rung to tell her she could collect her car any time after midday.

The sound of his voice had made her blood heat up.

Which was why she'd put off collecting her car until the last possible minute.

She adjusted her shirt and then pushed through to the interior of the office. A bell above the door gave a merry jingle. Photographs of classic cars lined the walls. There was no receptionist behind the desk again, but a glance at her watch told Blair that the receptionist would've already left for the day. As the sound of the bell died away the silence became stifling.

She cleared her throat. 'Hello?' Her voice came out high and thin, making her wince.

'Hey, Blair.'

Nick emerged from the door to her right. He'd

recently showered, his dark hair damp and his face freshly shaved. He wore jeans that sat low and hugged his hips, and a polo shirt that revealed whorls of crisp hair at its vee.

Yum. Her blood Mexican-waved in her veins. Her breasts tingled—even the right breast that wasn't there any more. Beneath her shirt one nipple puckered. The other...

She swallowed.

He frowned. 'You okay?'

He took a step forward. She took a step back. 'Yes, of course,' she lied, fighting the urge to rub her hand over her left breast—her real breast—to scrub the tingles away. She didn't know what to do about her right breast and the phantom sensations that attacked her. Scrubbing wouldn't help.

Dammit! She didn't want to want any man. Especially not Nick Conway. The memory of the horror on his face when she'd told him she wore a wig still made her flinch. That horror would only increase tenfold if he ever saw her naked.

And she wasn't putting herself through that. Not again.

She crossed her arms tight across her chest. They pressed her prosthetic breast hard against her scar, reminding her how different she was now.

But she was alive.

'I'm sorry.' She gestured to his freshly show-ered self. 'I've held you up.'

'Nah, you're right on time.'

He said that in a way that made her heart stum-ble. 'I…uh…what's the damage?'

He moved behind the reception desk, riffled through some papers, and then handed her an itemised account.

Her eyes widened when she read the total. 'You promised you were going to charge me premium rates. These look like mates' rates.'

One corner of his mouth kicked up. Her heart thumped all the way up into her throat as she watched the grin spread across those lean firm lips to crease his eyes.

'*Are* we mates, Blair?'

Could he have said that in a lower, huskier, more seductive voice if he'd tried? Mates… Mating. Seriously inappropriate images pounded through her.

'No!' And then she realised how that sounded. 'I mean…'

He threw his head back and laughed. 'You should've seen the look on your face, city girl. You need to lighten up a bit.'

He'd been teasing her? She waited for relief to flood her. It didn't. 'Yokel!' she shot back anyway, remembering their sparring from the other day and how much she'd enjoyed it.

He flicked the account she held. 'These are my usual rates. There weren't any problems with your car, no unusual parts that needed replacing.' He shrugged. 'That's what I charge.'

And then she saw the company name on the letterhead—Conway's Classic Car Restorations. He wasn't an ordinary run-of-the-mill mechanic. She bit back a groan. No wonder Glory's eyebrows had shot up yesterday when Blair had mentioned she was taking her car to Nick for a service. 'You restore classic cars?'

He didn't say anything.

She swallowed. 'You don't normally service regular cars, do you?'

'It's good to keep my hand in every now and again.'

Which, she understood immediately, wasn't an answer. Had he serviced her car out of *pity*?

Then she remembered he'd made the offer before she'd told him she'd had cancer.

'I wanted to make amends,' he said softly. His dark eyes travelled over her face, making her breath catch. 'For yelling at you and generally acting like a boor.'

So he'd done it out of guilt. Guilt was marginally better than pity, she supposed, but not by much. She didn't bother challenging him any further. She seized her chequebook and wrote him out a cheque as quickly as she could. Which wasn't all that quickly because he watched her so closely it made her hand shake.

She had to get out of here fast. Nick rattled her. He reminded her of the girl she'd once been. A girl who could flirt and laugh with a guy. A girl who'd felt comfortable in her own body. A girl who had once honestly believed that beauty was only skin deep.

That girl was long gone. She could never be that girl again. And remembering? That just hurt.

But she was alive. She had a lot to be grateful for. She couldn't forget that.

She handed him the cheque. He locked it in a strongbox before handing her the keys to her car. Only he didn't let go of them once she took them. His fingers brushed against hers, their warmth and vigour flooding her. She wanted to snatch her hand away, to stamp out the need that rose through her. Only that would be too revealing.

She gritted her teeth and kept hold of her half of the keyring.

'I want to apologise again for what happened last Sunday. For misjudging you like I did…and for the things I said.'

'Forget about it. I have,' she lied.

He still didn't let go of her car keys. His gaze refused to release hers. 'You said the other day that being sick made you feel like a freak?'

She dropped her hand. She folded her arms. 'I said the way people treat me since I've been sick makes me feel like a freak,' she corrected tartly.

'Blair, you're not a freak.'

She opened her mouth to tell him she already knew that, but the words wouldn't come. Whether it was right or wrong, in her heart of hearts a freak was exactly what she felt like.

'You've been through a rough time, but you are not a freak.' He stabbed a finger at her nose. 'And you shouldn't let anyone make you feel like one.'

He stared at her as if he could see into her innermost soul. Her stomach started to churn. She dragged her gaze away and told herself to stop being stupid.

'You might not be able to control how other people behave, but you can control your own reactions to them. People can only make you feel like a freak if you let them.'

His words raised gooseflesh, but she had no faith in them. 'Thanks for the lecture,' she drawled, hating the sarcasm that laced her every word but unable to do anything about it. It seemed she had two options available to her at the moment—sarcasm or tears—and she had absolutely no intention of crying.

She held out her hand. 'May I have my car keys?'

Nick hated the closed and shuttered expression that tightened Blair's face. He wanted to make her smile. He wanted the teasing and the banter back. He wanted to make her cheeks pink with awareness for him again.

The way her eyes darted away whenever their gazes clashed told him there was no problem on the awareness front, though. For either one of them—as the growing discomfort of his jeans testified.

He wanted to kiss her.

The thought made him back up a step. Instinct warned him that kissing her would end in tears. Eventually. Probably his. He had no intention of messing about with Blair. He had no intention of messing about with any woman. He might risk another relationship one day—he hadn't wholly given up on the idea of another marriage, of more kids—but he wasn't ready for all that yet. And certainly not with this woman.

Although he hadn't recognised it at the time, he could see now what a fragile state Sonya had been in towards the end of their marriage. Blair was recovering from cancer. He hadn't even asked her what kind of cancer—her expression the other day had forbidden such probing—but there was no mistaking that she was in a fragile state too. He didn't know if he could cope with another fragile woman. What if he let her down? He had enough guilt already—guilt that Sonya had died, guilt that Stevie had grown up without a mother. He wasn't ready to add another name to that list.

For heaven's sake, he'd known Blair for all of two minutes!

Somehow, though, they'd touched each other in ways painful to both of them, and in the process they'd caught sight of something that no one else had. He could tell himself what he liked, but that mattered.

'My keys?' she reminded him, her voice an ache of strain.

Before he could place them in her outstretched hand Stevie came racing into the office. 'Dad, Poppy doesn't have to babysit tomorrow now, so can we still go—?'

She pulled up short when she saw Blair. 'Hi, Blair.'

The shutters flew up from Blair's eyes. She sent Stevie the kind of smile that could nail a man's heart to the wall if he wasn't careful.

'Hi, Stevie.'

Her genuine delight at seeing his daughter melted a part of his brain and opened an ache up in his chest. He cleared his throat, wishing he could clear his head as easily.

'Dad?'

That was when he realised he was still staring at Blair. He forced his gaze to his daughter and gave a mock, world-weary sigh. 'So you want me to take you to Chichester Dam tomorrow, right?'

He obviously hadn't put enough of the mock into the sigh, because Stevie's face clouded. 'Do you have other plans? You said that you didn't have to work this weekend.'

'And I don't.'

Her face immediately cleared. There was some biology assignment or other that she was using as leverage to get him to take her and Poppy up into the Barrington Tops National Park. Not that she needed an excuse. He loved the national park as much as she did. 'Want to make a day of it?'

Her face lit up. 'Can we?'

'Sure. Why not? We'll take a picnic.' These were moments he treasured, when he could still glimpse the little girl in the teenager. She was worth every effort he had to make, and every sacrifice.

She grinned at him, and then her mouth formed an O and she spun to Blair. 'Blair, why don't you come too?'

Every muscle in Nick's body tensed. Hell, no!

'Maybe you could bring some scarves along to show me what you meant the other day and— I mean, only if you wanted to. It is gorgeous up there at his time of year and—' She broke off to scuff the toe of her shoe against the floor, her cheeks red. 'I guess you already know that, huh?'

His resistance dissolved. Just like that.

'Wow, Stevie, I haven't been up there in years.' Blair said it in exactly the right tone to disarm

Stevie's awkwardness. He could have hugged her for it.

Stevie's face grew eager again. 'So you'll come?'

'Well, I…'

She glanced at him. She didn't look any more enthused by the idea than he was. But for Stevie's sake… 'We'd love it if you joined us.' He wished there was more stoicism and less anticipation in his offer.

'I hadn't thought…'

He pushed her car keys into her hand. 'Perhaps you already have plans?' he rapped out, giving her the perfect excuse. This was a picnic, not a date. His anticipation worried him. It would be better if she stayed at home.

Something raced behind the backs of her eyes. 'May I bring Glory along? We'll contribute to the picnic hamper, of course.'

Glory? 'Sure. Why not? There's plenty of room. The more the merrier.'

She turned to Stevie. 'And you'd like me to bring along some scarves?' Stevie nodded eagerly. Blair turned back to him. 'What time should we be ready?'

'We'll collect you at ten o'clock.'

'Great! We'll see you then.' With a wave, she left the office.

'Isn't she something?' Stevie whispered, leaning into his shoulder as she watched Blair leave.

His lips twisted. That was one way of putting it.

Glory had jumped at the chance to come along on the picnic. Just as Blair knew she would because a) Glory wasn't working this weekend at the store—an art and craft cum antiques cum showcase-for-local-artists outlet that Glory and several other local women had formed a co-operative to run—b) Glory loved picnics, and c) she was bursting with curiosity about Blair and Nick.

Not that there was anything to be curious about. However, if her aunt thought a light flirtation was taking place, and was evidence of her improving health, then Blair was happy to go along with the pretence. This picnic would be another step in her scheme to prove to Glory that life should return to normal.

Nick collected them on the dot at ten. Blair sat in the back seat with the girls, insisting her aunt take the front seat. She did her best not to catch Nick's eye in the rearview mirror, but whenever she did he smiled at her, and she couldn't help but smile back.

Not that it meant anything.

But the sky was a matchless blue, and the sun shone with unparalleled enthusiasm, Glory's worry lines had started to fade and it suddenly seemed possible that everything could return to normal—to the way it had been before her cancer—and as far as Blair was concerned that was cause for smiling.

She might not be able to deny the spark of awareness that still arced between her and Nick, but it didn't worry her today the way it had when they'd been alone together in his office yesterday afternoon. They had two teenage girls and Glory acting as buffers today. The attraction might unsettle her, but nothing untoward could happen when she and Nick were part of such a crowd.

She told herself that was why it was so easy to relax, why it was so easy to flirt with Nick, and why he flirted back.

It was just a game.

That was *all* it was.

When Nick finally pulled the car to a halt, Blair unfastened her seat belt and leant forward to get a better view out through the front windscreen.

The breath left her lungs. Nick had chosen the most perfect spot—a clearing beside one of the many shallow streams that fed into the Williams and Chichester rivers. The grass, lush and green, beckoned, the water glistened silver as it trickled over the pebbles in the shallows, while the sun filtered down through the surrounding forest to dapple the clearing's edges with shade. In the deeper forest on the other side of the stream, tree ferns crowded under towering eucalypt and beech trees, and through their lacy fronds the green of moss gleamed.

Nick turned in his seat, and it was only then that she realised how far forward she'd shifted…and how close Nick's lips were to hers. She swallowed. This close, she could see his eyes were the colour of milk chocolate and that they were flecked with gold, like shards of honeycomb.

She'd bet kissing Nick would give her a bigger endorphin rush than chocolate.

'What do you think?'

'Beautiful,' she breathed, staring into those amazing eyes.

Glory cleared her throat and Blair snapped to, realising that Stevie and Poppy had already exited the car and were peering across the stream to a bush track that disappeared invitingly into the forest. Her cheeks burned, but she clapped her hands together. 'Let's get to it, then.'

She and Glory spread out a picnic blanket while Nick unloaded the car. He set up a camp chair for Glory and then raised an eyebrow towards Blair and lifted another chair. She shook her head and glanced away, her heart skittering around in her chest like a wild thing. 'I'll make do with the blanket.' He could have the chair, and hopefully he'd sit as far away from her as possible. She reached around him to grab the calico bag she'd brought along. Calling to the girls, she retreated to the blanket. They bolted over.

'Good God!' Nick stared as she strewed the bag's contents onto the blanket in front of her. She had a feeling he was doing his best to stop his lip from curling. 'There has to be at least a dozen scarves there.'

'Fifteen. I have neck scarves, square scarves, skinny scarves, winter scarves, and wrap scarves,' she said, tossing several to Stevie and Poppy.

He subsided to the other side of the blanket with a grimace. She did her best to ignore him as she showed the girls a variety of different ways to wear and tie a scarf, but she was aware of every restless movement he made, and the way his eyes rested on her for long brooding moments at a time. It made her hands less than steady.

Stevie made a frustrated sound in the back of her throat when, for the third time, she botched a layered knot—a style Blair had declared would particularly suit her. 'Can you show me step by step on Glory while I practise on Poppy?'

'I'm far too comfortable,' Glory announced before Blair could move her way. 'Use Nick as your model. His bones are younger than mine.'

'I'm not sure he could bear the challenge to his masculinity,' Blair said. She didn't want to get that close to Nick.

He slid across to her lazily, challenge alight in his eyes. 'Why don't we put that to the test?' And then he opened his legs wide, inviting her to kneel in the space between them, and her heart almost stopped.

She set her chin at a haughty angle, hoping it would hide the way her pulse raced. *Bluff! Don't let him know you're rattled.* She shuffled forward. She forced her gaze from honeycomb-flecked chocolate to glance at Stevie. 'Ready?'

At the younger girl's nod, she slid the scarf around Nick's neck.

'Loop the scarf so that the ends are hanging down Poppy's back and then bring them around like this.' Nick's neck was strong beneath her fingers and she tried not to let them linger against his warm flesh. 'Now, make sure the first loop is comfortable.'

She had to slide her fingers between Nick and the scarf. His quick intake of breath almost knocked her off balance. His gaze darkened and an ache started deep down inside her.

She wrenched her attention back to Stevie. 'Cross the ends over like this, and pull one of them through to make a second loop. Make the tail in front a bit longer so it hides the one at the back.' She forced herself to concentrate on Stevie's movements. 'Now, fold the first loop over the knot we've made so it covers it.'

'I got it!'

Blair immediately backed away from Nick on the pretext of checking Stevie's handiwork, but his knees closed about her hips, imprisoning her. 'I think you've forgotten something, princess.' He gestured to the scarf around his throat.

'But, darling.' She opened her eyes wide. 'It looks sublime on you.'

One corner of his mouth hooked up. With a low laugh, he released her. She checked Stevie's creation and pronounced it perfect, although she barely took it in. All she was aware of was Nick, and the way one of his large tanned hands dismantled the knot at his throat with ease.

'Masculinity still intact,' he said, handing her back the scarf. It was still warm. She dropped it before she could do something foolhardy like bury her face in it.

Glory pushed out of her chair. 'Girls, I'd love to see the spot where you saw the lyrebird last time you were here.'

'Coming, Blair?' Poppy asked. 'You wanted to see it too.'

'No, no.' Glory shook her head. 'Blair and Nick can busy themselves setting out the picnic things.'

Oh, good Lord! It was all she could do not to close her eyes. Aunt Glory was manufacturing an excuse for her and Nick to be alone. Self-preservation warred with her need to keep the charade up for her aunt's benefit. The latter won out.

'Maybe later,' she said to Poppy, winking at her aunt.

She and Nick watched in silence as their three picnic companions forded the stream and then set off down the bush track. He rounded on her as soon as the shade and undergrowth had swallowed them from sight. 'Why did you wink at Glory like that?'

'I didn't! I…uh…I had something in my eye.'

He shook his head. She couldn't tell if he was offended, vexed or amused. 'You're a rotten liar, Blair. You want Glory to think there's something going on between us, don't you?'

'Not precisely.'

He rested back on his hands, his lazy grin taunting her. 'Does that mean you *do* want to be alone with me?'

'No!'

He laughed.

She slumped. 'Look, Glory has been worried about me.'

'Of course she has.'

'Not ordinary worry. This has…grown. She's always fretting that I'm over-exerting myself, even when I'm doing the simplest things. She worries about me whenever I'm not here. She's talking about moving to Sydney to look after me.'

The air whistled between his teeth.

'You have to know as well as I do that Glory would be miserable away from Dungog and all her friends, and the store and her community work.' She listed the items off on her fingers. 'Why do you think I'm spending the next month here, Nicholas? It's to try and convince her that I'm well again.'

He frowned. 'She's not usually an alarmist.'

No, but... Blair swallowed. 'She thought I was going to die.' Even now, saying those words out loud could make her feel ill.

He stared at her, and then he dragged a hand down his face.

'Which is why I'm kicking myself for having made a rather stupid mistake.'

'Mistake?'

She stabbed a finger into the centre of one of the squares on the tartan rug. 'I run my own fashion label, okay?'

'Right.' He drew the word out.

'So I'm the boss, and of course I thought everything would go to rack and ruin if I wasn't there.'

'You went back to work too early?'

She grimaced. 'I fainted on the job. Everyone panicked, an ambulance was called…and so was Glory.'

He didn't say anything

'The crazy thing is I was fine. The doctors checked me over and released me the same day. But it was one scare too many for Glory.'

'She's been fretting ever since?'

Blair nodded and stabbed another square on the tartan rug. Then she lifted her head. 'But she's started to relax ever since she took it into her head that you and I have a…' she groped for an appropriate word '…*thing* happening.'

'So you want her to keep on thinking that this… *thing* is happening?'

'I just want her to see me having fun and being light-hearted, so that she can have fun and be light-hearted too.' She met his gaze, willing him to understand. 'Maybe then her fear will ease up a bit.' It was the only plan she had.

His face softened. 'She means a lot to you.'

'She means the world to me.'

He picked a piece of grass and twirled it in his fingers, but his gaze remained on her. It made her skin prickle.

'Stevie really enjoyed your class on Thursday night.'

Some of the tension eased out of her at the change of topic and she smiled. 'She's lovely. You must be very proud of her.' She tried not to notice the way his eyes lingered on her mouth.

'I am.'

He stretched out full-length on his side, head propped on one hand and his attention fully focussed on her. It took an effort of will to look away. 'You still don't approve of the Miss Showgirl quest, though, do you?'

His eyes narrowed. 'Let's get this straight. I do not think you're an air-headed narcissist, but…no, I don't approve of beauty pageants.'

She didn't bother telling him again that the Miss Showgirl wasn't just a beauty pageant. He wouldn't believe her anyhow.

Stevie had her father's support, but she didn't have his understanding, and Blair just didn't get it. She leant towards him. 'Why do you have such a bee in your bonnet about the Miss Showgirl quest? Why on earth do you hate it so much?'

He sat up. She didn't know how she could tell, but even though he maintained a casual posture, beneath it he was coiled up tight.

'Do you remember Sonya Blacklock?'

Sonya had been a couple of years behind Blair at school. She'd taken the modelling world by storm at about the time Blair had decided to quit. She might only vaguely remember Sonya from school, but she could recall Sonya's fate vividly.

Her mouth dried. 'She was your friend?' she croaked.

'She was my wife.'

If she hadn't been sitting she'd have fallen. She clutched a fistful of blanket. 'Wife?' she parroted. *But…* She leant forward. 'She was Stevie's…?'

'Mother? Yes.'

Air rushed into her lungs. 'Oh, Nick, I'm so sorry. I had no idea.' He didn't say anything. Her mind charged into overdrive. 'Sonya won the Miss Showgirl a couple of years after me,' she said slowly. 'Is that why you hate it? Because it reminds you of her?' Her heart burned. Did it remind him of all he had lost?

His eyes flashed and his nostrils flared. 'The world of fashion destroyed my wife. I hate it and everything it represents.'

Blair swallowed. He leant in close, his face dark. 'You want to know why I lost it that first day we met?'

His scent slugged into her. She dragged in a breath. He smelled healthy and clean, like soap. To lungs that had grown too used to the scent of sickness and disinfectant it was like manna. 'Why?' she croaked.

'Because Stevie made the fatal mistake of saying *"Blair Macintyre said…"*'

CHAPTER FIVE

'THAT'S all I heard the year before Sonya left. *Blair Macintyre this* and *Blair Macintyre that.* I heard when you were parading down the catwalks of Europe, Japan, New York. I heard when you became the face of some cosmetics company. I heard—' He broke off to drag a hand down his face.

Blair's jaw dropped. 'Sonya followed *my* career?' Blair's modelling career had been successful—and mercifully brief—but it had never been in the same league as Sonya's.

He flung out an arm. 'She was obsessed with you! As far as she was concerned if you could make it then so could she. I got sick to death of hearing your name.'

Blair could only stare.

'I know I overreacted, but to hear your name on Stevie's lips like that… It took me right back there.'

The expression in his eyes had her swallowing.

Those memories obviously weren't good ones. Then she frowned. If he and Sonya had been together when she was modelling... She cleared her throat. 'You guys must've married young.'

'High school sweethearts,' he said curtly. 'We married at eighteen and had Stevie six months later.'

Wow! Right.

He shook his head. 'We were too young. I can see that now. Sonya's obsession nearly bankrupted us. She'd spend the grocery money on clothes, jewellery, miracle face creams.' He dragged a hand down his face. 'It's not that I didn't want her to have pretty things, but—' His hands clenched. 'But back then money was tight, and there was Stevie to consider. It was all I could do to make ends meet.'

Silence opened up between them. Water trickled over pebbles. The raucous cry of a black cockatoo sounded in the distance.

Blair cleared her throat. 'Eventually Sonya's career took off, though,' she said tentatively. 'She would've been making good money.'

He didn't say anything. That was when it hit her. 'You didn't go with her? You stayed in Dungog when she left for the city?'

He nodded.

She moistened dry lips. 'Why didn't you go with her?'

He swung around, his gaze capturing hers. 'This is none of your business.'

Good Lord! What had she been thinking? 'I… No, of course it isn't. I'm sorry.'

His eyes didn't shift from her, and she had to fight the urge to fidget. She pointed to a random tree. 'Did you know that most of the interior of the Sydney Opera House was built from—?'

'Dungog brush box,' he finished, his lips twisting. 'Every local kid learns that in kindergarten, Blair. And, by the way, that isn't a brush box.' He nodded at her tree. 'It's a blue gum.'

Her ploy hadn't worked. Those knowing eyes continued to survey her from beneath heavy lids.

He had eyes that could tempt a hot-blooded woman to sin.

She forced her gaze away. Lucky she wasn't hot-blooded any more.

'If I tell you, city girl, then we're even stevens.'

She turned back, frowned. 'What are you talking about?'

He didn't say anything for a long moment. 'I know things about you that you'd rather I didn't.'

Like the fact that she'd had cancer.

'Quid pro quo. That's what I'm talking about. But when I'm done with my sorry tale the slate is clean. I no longer have to feel guilty about yelling at you, about misjudging you, et cetera, et cetera. We start again at square one.'

She pretended to consider it. 'I don't know.' She tilted her chin. 'If you promise to ditch the pity I'd consider it. But your guilt? I can always work that to my advantage.'

He stared. In the next instant he was flat on his back, roaring with laughter.

Mission accomplished!

He hauled himself upright again. 'I'm sorry you've been sick, Blair. But pity?' He shook his head. 'I don't think of you as weak or incapable.'

She wasn't sure she believed him.

'No pity and no guilt,' he offered.

'Deal,' she said, though she doubted he could rid himself so easily of either. She'd do what she could to hold him to his promise, though.

'So.' He leant back on his hands. 'The mistake that was mine and Sonya's marriage.'

Her stomach contracted. She wasn't so sure she wanted to hear this now.

'My father fell sick around the same time Sonya

and I found out she was pregnant.' He scratched a hand back through his hair. 'After that there was no more talk about going to university or travelling the world. My dream of eventually running a nature retreat so I could share all this…' he swept a hand around at the scenery '…disappeared into the ether. I started working full-time in the family business.'

'The automotive workshop?'

'I've been working there part-time since I was fifteen. I became a fully qualified mechanic in two years.'

Half the time it usually took. 'Impressive.'

'Necessary,' he countered.

'By then Stevie would've been…'

'Fifteen months.'

He stared up at the sky and Blair took the opportunity to drink in his features—the strong jaw, the slightly hooded eyes, and lips that were firm with promise. The blood in her veins quickened. She forced her gaze away.

'I promised Sonya that as soon as I was qualified and Dad was back on his feet we'd go to the city. I'd get work there and she could sign up with a modelling agency. I know we were too young to start a family. We discussed abortion, but a big family was all I'd ever really wanted. Sonya knew that and...' He hauled in a breath. 'I told her I'd stand by her, regardless of what choice she made, but I know it influenced her decision. I owed her.' He glanced at Blair. 'I meant to keep my promise.'

The tan had leached from his face. Her heart burned. 'What happened?'

'Everything was going as planned... And then Dad died.'

She sucked in a breath. 'Oh, Nicholas! I'm so sorry.'

'Mum was never the same again. I have four younger brothers. She needed help.'

She saw it all then. 'You stayed and ran the family business, helped your mother and put your brothers through school and university.'

He didn't turn to look at her. He didn't turn at all. 'There were five of them and one of Sonya. I didn't know what to do. In the end I let the math make the decision for me.'

He'd given up his dreams to ensure his siblings didn't have to give up theirs. He'd provided his family with the security and support they'd needed. But at what cost? It was obvious that Sonya hadn't managed to be as self-sacrificing. A part of Blair understood that too—that hadn't

been the life Sonya had signed on for—but her
heart burned for all that Nick had lost.

'You were both so young,' she whispered.

'I get why Sonya left. I really do. What I can't
forgive is the way she abandoned Stevie.' He
flung out a hand. 'I spent every spare moment I
could taking Stevie to Sydney so she could see her
mother, but Sonya became more and more elusive.
Sometimes she'd show up at the arranged meeting point. Other times she wouldn't. There would
never be an explanation or an acknowledgement.
She never returned to Dungog once to see Stevie.'

Or him. She wanted to reach out and touch him,
offer him comfort, but she suspected he would
merely shrug her off.

'Idiot that I was, I still thought I could save our
marriage. I still thought we could have that big
family.'

She closed her eyes.

'Until the morning a headline in a newspaper
told me she'd died of a drug overdose.' He gave a
harsh laugh. 'The reporter didn't even know that
she had a husband and a daughter. Neither did the
police until I contacted them.'

'Oh, Nick, I'm sorry.' Her voice came out a
hoarse whisper.

His knuckles turned white as he clenched his hands. 'I should never have made promises I couldn't keep. If I hadn't then maybe Sonya would still be alive today.'

She reached over and covered his hand with hers. 'Sonya had free will, Nicholas. Nobody was holding a gun to her head. And can you honestly say that you think she regretted having Stevie?'

He pursed his lips and then shook his head. 'She resented the ties that bound her to Dungog, and the way things turned out between me and her… but, no, I don't think she regretted Stevie.'

'And, Nicholas, the drugs…' Her hand tightened over his. 'They were nothing to do with you.'

He met her gaze. The shadows started to retreat from his eyes, and as they did his heat flooded into her. She tried to draw back, but he turned his hand over and his fingers closed around hers, capturing them fast. Her mouth dried.

'You're a good listener, Blair Macintyre.'

She should remove her hand from his. She should.

She squeezed his hand instead. 'You shouldn't give up on your dream of a big family.'

He let go of her hand then. 'Never let it be said that I don't learn from my mistakes.'

'Which means approaching a relationship with more maturity than you did in the past. It doesn't mean giving up on your dreams altogether.' A big family, that nature retreat—he shouldn't give up on those things.

Shutters slammed down over his eyes.

'You're what? Thirty-four?' she persisted.

'Drop it, Blair.'

'So there's still time.' Only that was what she had thought, wasn't it? Children certainly didn't figure in her future now. She cut the thought off. This was about him, not her.

He leant back, stretched his legs out in front of him, but she saw through the assumed nonchalance. 'I'm a bachelor guy these days. Footloose and fancy-free.'

'Jaded,' she countered.

The expression in his eyes warned her to back off. She decided to heed the warning. For now. Besides, they hadn't finished with the topic of his opposition and hostility towards the Miss Showgirl quest yet.

'So you hate the Miss Showgirl quest because it reminds you of Sonya's obsession with becoming a model.'

He didn't say anything.

'Does that mean because I was a model in the past, and because I'm a fashion designer now, it follows that I'm obsessive and irresponsible and the kind of person who'll take drugs?'

'I'm not saying that.'

'Yes, you are.'

'I—'

'You're also saying that if Stevie decides to become a model she will be as obsessive and irresponsible as her mother.'

His hands clenched. 'That world destroyed Sonya. I will not let it destroy Stevie too.'

'No, Nicholas, you're wrong.' She tried to make her voice soft to counter the hard truths she wanted to utter. 'Sonya destroyed herself. She let obsession and ambition rule her. It's not the modelling world that's to blame. It could as easily have been an obsession with becoming an Olympic athlete or a world-class ballerina or a property tycoon that drove her.'

'But—'

He broke off. He dragged both hands back through his hair. She noticed they weren't quite steady.

'I know you've lost a lot—both you and Stevie—and I'm really sorry about that. I truly am. But what happened to Sonya—that doesn't make the world of fashion bad or wicked. That's just your projection of it.'

He stilled.

'And Stevie's interest in pretty clothes and make-up and looking nice…well, that's just normal.' She held his gaze. 'You have to trust her. You have to trust that when the time comes she will make the right decisions for herself. If you don't, you'll damage your relationship with her.'

A scowl blackened his face. 'Have you ever been married?'

'No, I—'

'You don't have children!' he all but shouted.

Her throat closed over.

'So what makes you think that you're such an expert?'

She couldn't answer.

'I—' He broke off to turn away and pinch the bridge of his nose between thumb and forefinger. 'Sorry, I didn't mean to yell.'

She still couldn't speak.

His hand clenched. 'Look, what you're saying… it makes sense. But it's a lot to take in and…'

And it was obvious that no one had challenged his mindset before.

'I'm sorry,' he repeated.

'Forget about it,' she managed. She stared across at the stream until the burning in her eyes and throat had receded.

'City girl?'

'Yes?'

'Why haven't you married and done the kid thing?'

She glanced down at her hands, taken by surprise at the shaft of pain that speared into her. After everything he'd just revealed, though, she couldn't very well tell him to butt out. 'There have been a couple of long-term relationships that I thought…but they didn't work out.

Like Adam. She'd thought she and Adam would live the dream—beautiful house in the suburbs, a couple of golden-haired children, annual holidays abroad, together through thick and thin.

She'd been wrong. So *very* wrong.

He leant towards her. 'Princess, they must've been idiots.'

She glanced up…and drowned in the sight and scent of her picnic companion, at the expression in the warm brown depths of his eyes—sympathy, understanding, hunger. The pulse at the base of his jaw pounded. She watched that pulse, counted the beats, felt her own body quicken in answer and fall into tempo with it.

Ba-boom. Ba-boom. Surely he must hear it?

The expression in his eyes heated her flesh. The heat started in her neck, her cheeks, and then flashed down through the rest of her body, stealing her strength. Even though she'd promised herself that the warmth would not beguile her.

But the heat cascading through her now was like nothing she'd ever experienced, and Nick smelled of sun-warmed grasses and soap and cotton and it made her forget bad things. It made her remember she was only thirty-six.

He leant closer, slugging her anew with his scent and his heat. She could see a tiny nick on his chin where he must have cut himself shaving this morning. And still the pulse in his jaw pounded. His eyes darkened. His gaze dropped to her lips. Her breath caught and her lips parted the merest fraction. The merest fraction, perhaps, but he noticed.

His gaze lifted back to hers, his eyes dark and fiery. 'I'm going to kiss you, city girl.'

He wrapped a finger around a lock of her hair and she didn't even flinch.

'Why?' She reached up to press the flat of her palm against his cheek.

'Because you're beautiful.'

Not any more she wasn't. Even if his eyes told her otherwise. She moved her hand experimentally. Beneath her hand his skin was firm and hot. Her fingers prickled with the urge to explore further.

'And because I like you.'

Her mouth dropped open.

'And because I can't get the thought of it out of my head.'

Pity, she told herself as his lips swooped down to hers. This was a pity kiss.

And then all thought fled, because this was no tentative I-might-hurt-her kind of kiss. It was strong and sure and hungry, and it demanded that she take part or back off now. The strength of his passion knocked her preconceptions sideways. She hadn't meant this to go beyond a brief touch of the lips. But…

There were no kid gloves as he cupped her face with both his hands to drag her lips more fully against his, as his tongue swept across hers, daring her to dance and revel and enjoy. This was straight man-and-woman passion. No hiding, no games…*and no pity*. It was so heady and so liberating that Blair found herself kissing him back with a fervour she hadn't known she had.

She shuffled closer to him on her knees. Her hands crept around either side of his neck, revelling in the strong column of his throat. The short hair at his nape tantalised her palms. Her hunger built and built and he matched it, kiss for kiss, caress for caress, until she found herself needing to get closer and closer. She crawled right into his lap, straddling it. His hands caressed her backside as their bodies strained against the barriers of their clothes towards each other until there was barely an inch of space between them. And not once did they break the kiss.

Finally she had to drag her mouth away to draw much-needed air into oxygen-starved lungs. Nick pressed slow, drugging kisses to her neck, and she couldn't hold back a moan or the wanton way her body arched against his mouth.

It was magic, like Sleeping Beauty coming to life at her Prince's kiss. And she wanted more!

And then something wrong, out of place, made her still…

And then she realised what it was—her prosthesis. An alien and ugly thing, pressing against Nick's chest and her even uglier scar.

Blair flung herself off Nick's lap, unable to meet his eye as she readjusted her clothes with fingers that shook.

'What the hell…?'

'That shouldn't have happened.'

'I—'

'Glory, Stevie, and Poppy will be back any moment.'

'I—'

'Did you mean for it to go that far?'

'No, I…'

'You should get the Esky out of the car.'

When he didn't say anything she finally met his gaze. 'Please?' she whispered.

With a muttered oath, he rose to his feet. 'This is a reprieve. This discussion isn't over.' And then he stalked towards the car.

Blair closed her eyes. What had she been thinking? Her stomach churned. She thought she might actually be sick when she realised how close they'd been to tearing each other's clothes off. Had she really left herself open to—?

What if he'd seen her naked?

She flinched, recalling Adam's reaction—his rejection still so fresh and devastating. She couldn't go through that again.

Through the mash of her emotions, though, one thing became startlingly clear. Nick was actually attracted to her. It wasn't some lukewarm attraction either, but something smoking hot that could flare out of control.

And burn them both badly.

Need thickened her throat, billowed in her stomach, and just for a moment something golden shone in the darkness. Nick knew she wore a wig. He knew that beneath it she was bald. And yet he still wanted her.

For a moment she wanted to sing. She wanted to dance.

And then she wanted to weep.

This—them—it couldn't go anywhere.

Not today. Not next week. Not next month. Not ever. And although she'd known that in her heart as soon as Adam had walked away, and although it had become confrontingly real the first time she'd clapped eyes on the scar that had once been her breast, now—right at this very instant—it cut deep and hurt in a way it never had before.

After lunch, Blair taught the girls how to do the salsa. Nick wasn't sure how she managed it, but she took them from self-consciousness to budding confidence with nothing but a few well-chosen words, some judicious praise, and a goodly dose of laughter. She taught Poppy to strut and make the most of her height. She taught Stevie to undulate her hips in a way that would have had him grinding his teeth together if he thought of her dancing like that with a boy. Only he couldn't think of anything beyond Blair.

She was beautiful, vibrant…and she fired his blood.

His skin tightened. That kiss had left him reeling. And hungry for more.

A whole lot more.

His hands clenched. Blair was forbidden fruit. He should never have been stupid enough, unguarded enough, to have dared even the tiniest taste. Now that he had…

'Coming, Dad?'

He jerked around to find all eyes gazing at him expectantly. 'What?'

'We're walking down to the dam,' Stevie said with exaggerated slowness. 'Want to come?'

'Sure.'

The girls raced off straight away, with Glory ambling after them at a slower pace. Blair's face fell. He waited to see if her need to avoid him was greater than her good manners.

Good manners won out. With a sigh, she knelt back down to the blanket and started packing away their lunch things.

When everything was packed up they set off after the others. Nick cleared his throat. 'About that kiss, Blair.'

Her chin lifted. 'I really rather we didn't discuss it.'

He chewed that over for a moment. The way she gripped her hands together, clenched and unclenched her fingers, was at odds with the tone of her voice. He cleared his throat and pushed on. 'I'm sorry. I didn't mean it to go so far.'

She didn't say anything.

'I...' He hated the awkwardness. He hated the mixed signals he kept sending this woman. He pulled her to a halt. 'I just want to make sure that you haven't got the...uh...wrong impression.'

She stared, and then she planted her hands on her hips. 'You'd better explain that.'

He rolled his shoulders. 'I didn't mean for the kiss to go as far as it did. I lost my head. And...I— uh—I didn't mean to give the impression that I'm in the market for anything serious or—'

Her snort cut him off short. 'You have tickets on yourself, country boy, if you think one kiss can turn my head.'

He grimaced. 'I put that badly. I just wanted us to be on the same page, that's all.'

'Oh, we're on the same page, all right. But just to make things crystal-clear—a relationship is the last thing I want right now. A fling is even further down my scale of priorities.'

He could understand her wanting to find her feet again after everything that she'd been through.

She hitched her chin up. 'And even if I was interested in something longer term, you are the last man I'd consider having that relationship with.'

His head shot up at that. 'That's a bit harsh.' She'd been as into that kiss as him. She couldn't deny they had chemistry.

'You want to believe you're some fancy shmancy, footloose and fancy-free bachelor, Nicholas, but you're not. At heart you're a family man.'

His blood started to run cold.

'And deep down you still want that big rambunctious family.'

His hands clenched. He knew she was right. Despite what he'd told her, he hadn't given up on that dream. Not totally. But the next time he took the plunge into matrimony—*if*—he meant to take his time and make sure he and his prospective partner shared the same values and world view, that they wanted the same things…that they had what it took to weather the tough times. *If* there was a next time, he meant to get it exactly right.

So far he hadn't found that kind of conviction or certainty with any of the women he'd dated.

'You and me, we're chalk and cheese, Nicholas. We want different things. A big bustling family?' She shook her head. 'I am the last woman on the planet who would be up for that.' Lines of strain fanned out from her eyes and her mouth, at odds with her tone of voice.

He folded his arms. 'Why not?' He didn't know why he asked, why he felt the urge to argue with her, only that something didn't feel right.

She cocked an eyebrow. 'Well, for starters, chemotherapy is pretty lethal to a woman's fertility.'

His head rocked back in shock. She tried to smile but he saw the effort it cost her, and his heart broke for her then—for all she'd suffered and for all she was still suffering. 'Blair, I'm sorry.'

She shrugged. 'It's not your fault.'

He hesitated. 'You know, there are other ways—adoption, IVF.'

'Don't, Nicholas. Please…just don't.'

Her pain cut at him.

'I'm thirty-six and single. And I don't want to be a single parent.'

'But you could meet someone!'

She dragged in a breath that made her whole body shudder. He saw then that for some reason she had discounted the idea of a romantic relationship from her future. Why?

'I'm happy with what I have, and that will have to suffice.' She raised an eyebrow. 'So, now we know that we're both on the same page. Right?'

His shoulders slumped. 'Right.' He straightened and slung an arm around her shoulders to propel them forward again, wanting to do what he could to wipe the darkness from her eyes. 'You have no rules against friends, though, have you?'

'None at all,' she whispered.

'Well, that's okay, then.'

Only it felt like the least okay thing in the world.

CHAPTER SIX

NICK glanced up from his spot at the kitchen table to check the wall clock. The big hand had only moved a couple of millimetres from the last time he'd checked. It was Thursday night, and the second of Blair's classes. He gave up pretending to do the accounts. He gave up lying to himself. For all the good it would do him, he wanted to know how Blair was doing—how she looked, if she was happy. He wanted to pump Stevie and Poppy for every titbit they could feed him the moment they walked through the door.

But it had only just gone eight o'clock. The class would run for another thirty minutes yet, and it was far too early to walk across to the showground to escort the girls home. He rubbed the back of his neck. Besides, Stevie would kill him if he did that. She and Poppy were walking back here together. It was the deal he'd struck with them. They'd walk home together, and Poppy would either stay over or he'd run her home. They were at that age where it was way too uncool to be collected by a parent. They were at that age where they were fighting for more and more independence.

He got that. He really did. But he still considered running the gauntlet of teenage wrath if it meant he could manage just a glimpse of Blair. The girls were sixteen, caught up with their own concerns. They wouldn't notice if Blair was down or not. And he wanted to know how she was doing.

He drummed his fingers against the table. He could always ask her out to dinner. A friendly dinner. And—

He bit back a curse and leapt up to pace around the table. Dinner would lead to other things. He slashed a hand through the air. Blair and him—it would never work.

Why not?

He sat back down. Blair was generous. She gave to other people. He liked her. He liked her a lot. He admired her courage, relished her quick mind, and one sultry glance from those baby blues could send his blood pressure rocketing skywards. But…

She'd made it clear she wasn't interested in pursuing a relationship. He wasn't either. But suddenly that sentiment seemed empty and meaningless. He moistened suddenly dry lips. If he was ready…?

He shied away from the thought. Blair had been through a lot. She needed this time to focus on herself, not a relationship. He understood that entirely.

That didn't prevent regret from swirling through him, churning his stomach with what-might-have-beens. It didn't stop his skin from tightening whenever he thought about her.

And there was no denying it. He thought about her a lot.

Even though nothing serious could happen between them.

He shifted on his chair, adjusted jeans that suddenly felt too tight. What about something not-so-serious, then, like a holiday romance?

The thought had barely formed before he shook it away. Blair had said she didn't want a fling either. Even if he could change her mind it would get too complicated. Besides, he owed her the courtesy of heeding her wishes. He had no intention of complicating her life just because he had an itch to scratch.

He glanced at the clock again and then leapt to his feet. Eight-fifteen. Stevie and Poppy could grumble all they liked. He might as well burn for catching a glimpse of the woman as not, and—

He spun around when the front door slammed. Stevie and Poppy stomped down the hallway towards the kitchen. 'God, Dad, you won't *believe* what happened. It sucks!' Stevie said the moment she appeared.

'Ferociously!' Poppy added.

They threw themselves down into chairs. He took one look at their slumped shoulders and disgruntled faces, and put the kettle on. Hot chocolate was obviously in order.

He sat too. 'Tonight's session didn't go well, then?'

Stevie's face lit up. 'The class was brilliant!'

That lighting up twisted his gut with love for his little girl. Not-so-little girl, he amended. He would do anything to keep that expression on her face for ever.

'Blair talked about the importance of good posture.' Both girls immediately straightened. 'You really shouldn't slouch like that, Dad. It's not good for your health.'

He made himself push his shoulders back and sit straighter. When both girls nodded their approval it was all he could do not to leap up and hug them. They were so young, so full of life and hope.

'We practised our posture—sitting, standing, and walking,' Poppy added. 'Blair told us how important it is in job interviews and stuff. Our posture sends out a message to people.'

It had made a difference to Poppy already. She had a tendency to hunch her shoulders and hunker down in her seat, as if to compensate for her height. But she was sitting tall and proud at the moment. For the first time he glimpsed something more than just a beauty contest. As Blair had told him he would.

There's nothing wrong with a woman wanting to make the most of herself.

He'd thought Blair had been talking about clothes and make-up. It hit him now that she'd been talking about something more than that, like attitude and confidence and taking care of yourself.

'Sounds great. So if the session was so good why the long faces?'

Both sets of shoulders slumped. That sent out a definite message.

'They've replaced her.'

'Who?' He glanced from one girl to the other. 'Who's replaced who?'

'Blair! The committee have replaced Blair with Mabel Fowler.'

He shot to his feet. 'But…but Glory's on the committee.' They couldn't replace Blair!

'Glory runs a craft club up at the nursing home on a Thursday night. She wasn't there.'

He couldn't believe what he was hearing. 'But… why?'

'Because she's not a member of the show committee.'

Since when had *that* ever mattered?

'And because apparently she's been sick and they think it's too much for her to take on.'

His heart sank to his feet. He dropped back to his chair. All she wanted to do was to get her life back on track and yet nobody would let her.

Stevie swallowed. 'She was so gracious and polite.'

'Her posture was beautiful as she left.' Poppy sniffled.

'She wished us all well, told us we were all beautiful and that we'd do the Miss Showgirl quest proud this year.'

Both girls promptly burst into tears.

Nick placed a box of tissues into the middle of the table. He made steaming mugs of hot chocolate and patted shoulders until the storm had passed.

'I think it sucks ferociously too,' he said, once they'd blown their noses and dried their eyes. 'Now, drink your hot chocolate.'

If Glory was out for the evening it meant Blair would be home alone.

'Will you girls be okay if I go out for a bit?'

'Daaaaddd.' Stevie rolled of her eyes. 'We're sixteen, you know.'

He took that as a yes. 'Well, don't stay up too late? It's a school night.'

Both girls smiled at that, and called out goodnights as he let himself out through the door.

Damn that meddling committee. Their meddling would have been well-intentioned, but…

Why hadn't they spoken to Glory first?

A nasty thought slithered through him. Maybe they had. Maybe Glory thought it was all too much for Blair too?

Maybe they were right?

He flashed back to the woman on the picnic last Saturday. Sure, there was a certain vulnerability to her, a fragility…but she'd kissed him with a passion that had set him alight. She'd taught the girls how to salsa. Sure, she'd been breathing hard at the end of it, but so had Stevie and Poppy. They'd hiked. And she'd eaten with as healthy an appetite as any of them.

Blair had been sick. Obviously. Terribly sick. But she was well on the road to recovery now, and she had every right to live her life the way she saw fit. Without interference from anyone else.

He hated what she must be going through right now.

He tapped on her back door. He counted to ten and then knocked again, harder this time.

'Nicholas?'

He spun around to find Blair standing behind him. 'Stevie and Poppy told me what happened,' he said without preamble. 'I wanted to make sure you were okay.'

Blair didn't want her heart to lurch and swoon in her chest at the sight of Nick. But her heart, it seemed, had a mind of its own.

A rather wayward mind at that—reckless and wilful.

Won't do either one of us any good, she warned it. She had a feeling that if her heart could grow arms and a face it would thumb its nose at her about now. The image made her want to smile.

No, it was the sight of Nick that made her want to smile.

That realisation wiped the desire to do any such thing right off her face. She and Nick couldn't be anything more than friends.

A week spent pondering how to make her car break down so she could take it to Nick for repair, to give her an excuse to see him, wasn't being just friends.

It was being pathetic!

'Where have you been?'

It wasn't until he spoke that she realised the length of the silence that had stretched between them. She was glad of the night and the dark, because heat suddenly rushed into her cheeks. She had a feeling she'd been standing there feasting on the sight of him like some hungry child with its face pressed against the plate-glass window of a cake shop.

'I went for a walk.' She'd been too keyed-up to come straight home.

She edged past him, careful not to touch him. She didn't need the rush of warmth, the jolt of electricity that touching him would fire through her. Her heart was acting ridiculously enough without letting her brain follow suit.

'It was nice of you to drop by to check on me, Nicholas. You'd better come in.'

She'd left the kitchen light on. When they entered and she turned back to glance at him her breath caught at the way the golden glow glinted from the lighter tips of his rich dark hair, creating a halo effect around his head. The light contrasted with eyes that were almost black at the moment. A dark-eyed angel—who was concerned for her.

She gestured for him to take a seat at the table. 'Tea, coffee?'

'Can you stretch to hot chocolate?'

She seized a box of cocoa. 'That I can.' She put a saucepan of milk on to boil. She tore open a packet of marshmallows and popped one into her mouth, set them on the table, and gestured for Nick to help himself.

Neither one of them said anything. It wasn't a hard silence. In fact it was kind of nice. She appreciated the company. It allowed the fury of her thoughts to settle for a bit while she focussed on playing host.

She spread half a dozen Tim Tams onto a plate, poured boiling milk into the cups, and carried it all across to the table. She dropped two marsh-mallows into her mug. Nick followed suit.

'Do you remember doing this as a kid?' She bit off one corner of her Tim Tam and then turned it around and bit off the opposite corner as well. She then stuck the biscuit in her mug of hot choc-olate as if it were a straw, and sucked. Hot choco-late and melted chocolate biscuit hit her in a rush and she groaned in bliss. 'I haven't done that in for ever.'

Nick grinned. He picked up a biscuit too, but bit into it straight away. 'Best biscuits in the world.'

She nodded, polishing off hers and licking her fingers. And then she reached for another marsh-mallow and demolished it too.

'You know, whenever I see Stevie with this amount of chocolate and sugar it clues me in that she is either hormonal or has had a really bad day at school.'

'I'm not hormonal.'

He nodded, and they drank in silence for a bit.

'Besides,' she finally said, 'I'm sick and tired of being so darn healthy. Research has shown that bitter greens are very good for the kidneys and liver, which get knocked around during chemo. So I've been eating lots of bitter greens. It's just...'

'That they're bitter?'

She pointed a half-eaten Tim Tam at him. 'Exactly. And a girl should be allowed an occasional chocolate breakout. It's only right and fair.'

'Absolutely.'

Done with her momentary bout of self-pity, she pushed her shoulders back. 'How are the girls? They looked pretty shell-shocked when the committee came in and announced they'd found a replacement mentor.'

'They're angry...disappointed.'

She stared at the tabletop, drew imaginary patterns across it with her finger. 'I can't help feeling I've let them down.'

'*You?*'

She thought he was going to leap up and start pacing, but finally he slumped back in his chair.

'The committee should be shot for making such a stupid decision. Did you try to reason with them?'

'They didn't really give me the opportunity.' As far as they were concerned it had been a *fait accompli*. 'And it was hard in front of the girls.' She hadn't wanted to make a scene. She'd been afraid she might cry. 'I was only ever a temporary mentor.' She hadn't expected to be quite so temporary, though.

He scowled. 'But—'

'And I've discovered that it's very difficult to fight or reason with kindness,' she cut in, not wanting to hear what he had to say. She'd said it all to herself on her walk already. 'There's a certain self-righteousness behind it…' She shook her head. 'People don't want to believe that their good intentions can, in fact, have a less than good impact.'

This time he did leap up. 'Bunch of meddling turkeys!' And then he seemed surprised to find himself on his feet. Muttering, he took his empty mug to the sink and rinsed it.

He leant back against the sink, his legs crossed at the ankles. She swallowed. Long, lean legs. She remembered their strength against the backs of her thighs when she'd straddled them on Saturday.

When she'd kissed him with a passion she'd thought she'd lost for ever.

'Blair, Glory is on the committee.'

Oh, good Lord, stop staring! Heat surged into her cheeks and she dragged her gaze from Nick to doodle idly on the tabletop again. Then his words sank in. Glory? She bit back a sigh.

'Do you think she knew what was going to happen tonight?'

The same question had been swirling through her head since she'd left the hall at the showground. Had Glory known that the committee meant to replace her? She suspected the answer was yes. She suspected Glory was behind the move. But…

She'd thought she'd been making inroads where Glory was concerned. She'd thought she'd been making progress. Good progress, in fact.

Except…

She swallowed. Except every time Glory had raised the subject of Nick and the picnic Blair had promptly changed the subject. She closed her eyes. Exactly how much moping had she done over Nick this week? And what had Glory read into it?

She slammed her empty mug onto the table with a solid, satisfying bang. 'Damn it, Nicholas! I don't know what more I can do.' She leapt up and paced, in an attempt to expend some of the energy coursing through her. Nick watched her with hooded eyes, and that didn't help either. She flung an arm out. 'Do you know I spend nearly an hour every morning to make myself look like this? To make myself look normal so that people will treat me like I'm normal? And yet they still think I'm incapable of running a two-hour session each week for teenage girls!'

His jaw dropped. 'An *hour*?'

'Oh, yes!' She gave a laugh that lacked mirth. 'Long gone are the days when I could tug a comb through my hair, slick on a bit of lippy, and dash out the door.'

'An hour?' he repeated.

'And you're talking to a woman who can do a full evening face in under ten minutes.'

She folded her arms and glared at him. He looked flabbergasted. Not that she blamed him.

'I take it that's some mean feat, city girl?'

'You bet your darn patootie, you rustic.' But she found she was grinning as some of the frustration eased out of her.

He still leant against the sink, those legs of his still crossed at the ankles. He epitomised latent power. Strength and vigour practically breathed from his pores. His skin glowed with rugged good health, and as his eyes fixed on her face they glittered. For the life of her she couldn't look away. Power, strength, and vigour with a dash of devil-may-care danger thrown in. The mixture was intoxicating.

'Blair, what kind of cancer did you have?'

Those dark eyes refused to release hers. *What kind of cancer?* The air squeezed out of her lungs. It was almost refreshing to find someone who didn't know all the ins and outs of her illness. But it was still awful to say the words out loud.

She dragged air into her straining lungs, moistened dry lips. 'Breast cancer.'

He blinked. Surprised at her bluntness, perhaps, or surprised at the disease? She didn't know which, and she didn't want to know. But the blink had at least released her from his thrall. She dragged her gaze away and lowered herself back to her seat. She didn't want to watch his gaze lower to her chest. She didn't want to see the pity in his eyes.

She lifted her chin, but she looked past him at the wall. 'Breast cancer is the most prevalent cancer in Australian women after skin cancer.'

'Hell, Blair!' His voice was rough. 'Are you going to be okay?'

'I've had a mastectomy.' She gestured to her right breast. 'And chemotherapy. The doctors are confident that I'll make a full recovery. Officially

I won't be considered cancer-free for another five years. But, as I said, the prognosis is good.'

He uncrossed his ankles to lean forward. 'Maybe your aunt and the show committee and the people you work with are right. Maybe you *should* be taking it easy and—'

'Don't you dare!' She shot to her feet and stabbed a finger at him. 'I've had over four months of being mollycoddled. There is absolutely no medical reason why I cannot work. There's no conceivable reason why my life can't get back to the way it was before I was diagnosed with breast cancer.'

Minus one breast, of course.

And some hair.

And one boyfriend.

'Don't you *dare* join the ranks of those I'm fighting. If you cross the floor you are no longer my friend.'

He moved to the table in one fluid movement, his eyes dark and flashing, his mouth hard and compressed. 'Are you sure you're ready for all that?'

'Yes!'

'And that you're not pushing yourself too hard, too fast?'

'I'm positive.' The words ground out of her as

frustration bubbled up through her again. Why did everyone have to treat her as if she was going to keel over at any moment? 'What?' she suddenly shouted at him. 'I've lost a breast so that suddenly translates into becoming a totally irresponsible person? How stupid do you think I am? What conceivable reason would I have to jeopardise my health now, after all I've been through? Why would I even risk that?'

He scowled. 'All right. Keep your hair on!'

And then he blanched. Blair clapped both hands over her mouth, but a strangled laugh escaped her all the same. 'That is such an un-PC thing to say to someone who has just had chemo.'

'God, I'm sorry! I—'

Whatever else he said was lost in Blair's sudden attack of the giggles. The look on his face didn't help, and she fell back into her seat and howled with growing mirth. *Keep her hair on?* She and her fellow patients in the oncology unit had developed something of a gallows sense of humour, and although she knew Nick hadn't meant his remark literally it reminded her of the very bad jokes they'd used to make...of the courage of the women who had helped to buoy her spirits, and whose spirits she'd helped buoy in return.

She wiped her eyes and lifted her chin. 'People hate being reminded of death and their own mortality—that's what I do. People would prefer it if I stayed home, where they wouldn't have to see me and where they wouldn't be reminded about unpleasant things.'

'Blair, I—'

She held up a hand. 'I don't care how hard you make this for me, Nicholas—you, Glory, and all her friends—I *will* beat the lot of you.' She would! The lingering laughter dissolved. *She had to.* If she didn't then everyone would keep treating her and seeing her as a freak.

What hope would she then have of ever feeling normal again?

Nick sat with a hard thud. 'I'm not trying to make things hard for you. Breast cancer.' His hands clenched to fists. 'You said the words and I panicked. I'm sorry for underestimating you, for treating you as if you don't know how to look after yourself. I know all I ever seem to be doing is apologising to you, Blair, but I am *really* sorry if I made you feel undermined.'

'Thank you,' she said simply. His sincerity meant a lot. 'So...you'll help me, then?'

'In whatever way I can.' He shifted. His hands

unclenched. 'Did you have anything specific in mind?'

'Not really.' She sighed. 'If we had an affair it'd get everyone seeing me differently.' She stiffened. 'Not that I'm suggesting we do that, you understand. That would be a bad idea, but...' She trailed off and prayed her cheeks weren't as red as she suspected they might be.

'We could pretend.'

'No, I don't want to lie. I just want everyone to stop seeing me as an invalid.'

He suddenly leant forward. 'Fun and healthy.'

'What?'

'You have to let people see you having fun and looking healthy.'

She gestured to her hair and face. 'I thought I was taking care of the *looking* part.'

He snapped his fingers. 'Can you play softball?'

'Sure I can. But it's been a while.'

'Stevie's school is having a parents and friends softball and sausage sizzle day this Sunday, to raise money for sports equipment. I mean, there'll be more activities than just softball, but...'

'You want me to come and play softball?'

'I want you to show everyone that you can run, hit a ball, and have a laugh.'

The beauty of his plan hit her. 'That's perfect!' If she wanted people to treat her as if she was normal, she needed to start acting as if she was normal. Bluff, remember? And who knew? Maybe feeling normal would naturally follow. Eventually. 'And perhaps being seen at the local pub on a Friday or Saturday evening wouldn't hurt either.'

'Excellent,' he agreed.

'I could drag Glory to the movies.' Dungog boasted one of the oldest purpose-built cinemas in the state.

Nick clapped his hands and then leant back in his seat, smug self-satisfaction stretching across his face. 'You could go freelance.'

Okay, he'd lost her now.

'You could offer classes…' he pursed his lips '…twice a week.'

'On?'

'All that girly stuff—how to present yourself and…and…stuff.'

She grinned at his floundering, but… Grooming and deportment classes? Did she dare? 'I thought you disapproved of all that?'

'I…uh…' He scratched his head. 'Stevie and Poppy raved about tonight's class.' He rolled his eyes. 'Who knew posture could excite sixteen-year-old girls so much?'

'And who knew talking fast-bowling techniques and defensive batting strategies could do the same for sixteen-year-old boys?'

His eyes warmed, and then he shifted on his chair. 'Okay, confession time. Listening to the girls talk tonight, I finally glimpsed what you've been talking about. The Miss Showgirl thing *isn't* just about being thin and pretty. It's about an attitude. It's about building confidence and self-esteem. It's about...' He leant forward and frowned, as if searching for the right words. 'It's about the girls having belief in themselves and doing the best they can.'

His confession touched her.

'I can see now that wanting to be part of the quest doesn't mean any of them want to be models any more than...than the boys who play weekend cricket think they're going to make the Australian cricket team.'

'Bingo, country boy,' she said softly, her insides warming at his new understanding. 'The quest gave me the confidence to pursue a modelling career. And when I didn't find modelling all that satisfying I had the confidence to change career paths. The Miss Showgirl quest opened up avenues for me rather than closing them. For me, it was never about winning, and for most of the girls that holds true too. It's about pushing yourself, trying your best, and feeling proud of what you've achieved.' She grinned then, and gave a shrug. 'And it also happens to be a lot of fun.'

The warmth in his eyes didn't dissipate; it became more intense. 'Blair, you have a lot to offer those girls. I bet that if you ran the classes all the Miss Showgirl entrants would join up—plus others.' He pulled his wallet out of his back pocket. 'I'll pay for Stevie and Poppy right now.'

'Wait! Put that away.' She waved her hands at him. 'I'm only in town for another three weeks.'

'That's six classes—which is on par with the length of a short course at the community college.'

'But where would I run them? Here is too small.'

She could see him turn the matter over in his mind. 'What about the arts and crafts room at the back of the co-operative?'

That would work.

'Would they let you use it?'

'I'm ninety-nine per cent sure they would.' Glory might be worried about her, but Blair doubted she'd give a definitive no to her only niece. Not for renting a room at the store, where she'd feel she'd be able to keep an eye on Blair. 'Especially if I offered them a nominal fee for room hire.'

'And you have to charge.'

His commanding tone made her blink. 'Nicholas, I don't need the money. I was going to do it for free for the show committee.'

He stabbed a finger down onto the table. 'People won't take you seriously if you don't charge.'

'Fine! Five dollars a class, then.'

'Ten dollars.'

'I—'

'You can give the profits to charity, Blair, but I won't let you short-change your skills or yourself.'

She could give the profits to the Breast Cancer Foundation. Somehow that plan seemed perfect.

'I'll get Stevie to put a notice up on the school noticeboard.'

'I'll put one in the window of the store. In fact, I'll do a run of handouts along the main street. I'll clear the use of the room with Glory the minute she gets home.'

'If there's a problem with that, call me.'

'There won't be a problem.' She couldn't explain her confidence, only that this felt righter than anything had in an age.

As right as kissing Nick had felt.

She tried to push that memory out of her head before her heart starting jumping and swooning again.

She gulped. Too late for that. She did what she could to stop her brain from melting to mush instead. 'Thank you.' She went to touch his hand, but pulled back at the last minute. Better not.

'I haven't done anything except try to make amends.'

'Well, you've done it beautifully.'

His gaze lowered to her lips, and that heat arced between them. They both stilled, as if waiting.

And then Nick shoved his chair back. 'I should go. It's…uh…getting late. And it's a school night.'

'Wouldn't want you running late for class in the morning,' she drawled, rising to her feet too and leading the way to the back door.

'I understand princesses need their beauty sleep.'

She grinned. 'And their Tim Tams and hot chocolate. Goodnight, Nicholas.'

'Night, Blair.'

He walked out into the night and she tried to ignore the thrum of disappointment that gripped her when he didn't kiss her—not even a peck on the cheek.

She went to close the door, but he suddenly turned back. 'Blair, about Glory... She doesn't think of you the way you described everyone else.'

'I know.' Her heart ached. 'She's scared, terrified.' Which was why Glory was so careful and protective of her. She jerked up her chin. 'Which is why I mean to hang around for a long time yet.'

'I've been thinking. That hour it takes you to do your hair and make-up every morning—that might be one of the things worrying her.'

She frowned and edged closer, trying to see his expression in the darkness. 'You think I need to speed it up?'

'I don't think it's the length of time that's the problem, but your need to do it in the first place.'

And then he was gone out into the night, leaving her with more to ponder than when he'd arrived.

CHAPTER SEVEN

GLORY returned home a quarter of an hour after Nick had left. 'Hey, Aunt Glory,' she called as her aunt let herself in via the front door. 'I'm making chamomile tea. Want one?'

She needed something to soothe and settle her, calm her nerves after all that sugar.

She needed something to calm her after that dose of Nick, never mind the sugar. His presence fired her to life in a way that no man had ever done before. His effect on her was like red drink to a toddler.

And in large doses, just as lethal to sleep and peace of mind, she suspected.

Which was why she'd put the chocolate and marshmallows away and had settled for something herbal.

'I might head straight to bed, love. I'm tuckered,' Glory called out, not even sticking her head around the kitchen door.

Blair's shoulders slumped. Her head dropped.

Glory's uncharacteristic retreat told her that she had indeed been behind Blair's removal from being mentor to the quest entrants. *Oh, Glory!*

She lifted her chin. She jiggled her teabag. 'Before you rush off, I have a favour to ask.'

Silence. And then Glory appeared in the doorway, visibly nervous. Blair's heart clenched. She loved her aunt with all her heart. Plus more. Glory had taken her in when Blair was only eight, after her parents had died in a car accident. She had loved Blair unconditionally. She'd given Blair security, support, and stability. She'd made sure that they'd laughed together and had fun together. Blair's adolescence could have been a nightmare. Glory had ensured it wasn't.

Blair ached to see her aunt calm, relaxed, and happy again, instead of worrying, fretting, and fearing.

Making herself old.

It would take more than a cup of chamomile tea to achieve that, though.

Glory's gaze skittered away. 'How did your meeting go this evening?'

'Really well.' She'd promised herself not to bring the topic up unless her aunt did. 'The girls are all lovely and eager.'

Glory said nothing.

Blair squeezed out her teabag and turned to face Glory fully, nursing her mug between hands that felt chilled. 'I wanted to ask you a favour,' she started, determinedly cheerful. 'Would you and the other women at the co-operative consider renting me the art and craft room on Thursday nights and Saturday mornings for the next three weeks? I'll make sure I'm out of there before the Saturday afternoon embroidery club starts.'

Glory's hands knitted together. 'What do you want it for?'

'Oh, if it isn't convenient I can rent the training room at the library, but I'd rather the co-operative receive the room rental, that's all,' she replied, deliberately evading her aunt's question.

'Of course you can use the room, Blair, love. You don't need to pay rent.'

'Of course I'll pay.' She swooped down and planted a kiss on her aunt's cheek. 'Thank you. I want to run some deportment and personal grooming classes—a how-to-present-yourself-to-the-best-advantage class...maybe even a bit of fashion design. Working with the Miss Showgirl entrants has fired me up. I've really enjoyed it.'

'But—'

When her aunt didn't continue, Blair didn't press her. 'You're looking tired, Aunt Glory. You work too hard. Sorry, I didn't mean to keep you up. If you want to have a lie-in in the morning I'll do your shift at the store.'

'I don't need a lie-in!'

Blair bit back a grin. 'I was only offering, that's all.' She lifted her mug. 'I'll think I'll take this to bed with me.'

'Blair?'

She turned. 'Hmm?'

'Did the…um…committee show up at your meeting this evening?'

'They did.'

'And?'

'And they asked me to step down from my role as mentor and brought along a replacement. You know, I thought the excuse they gave about me not actually being a member of the committee was kind of petty and parochial…a bit narrow-minded.'

'Oh, dear!' Glory's hands fluttered to her cheeks. 'I hope you weren't offended.'

'I was, actually.' Then she took pity on her aunt. 'I do, however, think it's a valid point that the girls have the continuity of one mentor for the entire three months. Anyway, now it means I can run my own courses without the pressure of the quest hanging over my head. I can just have some fun. Goodnight, Aunt Glory.'

Her aunt's faint and bemused 'Goodnight, dear' followed Blair down the hallway. She found that she was smiling by the time she reached her bedroom door.

By four-thirty on Friday Blair had sixteen girls signed on for her course. On impulse, as she was walking past Nick's workshop on her way to the store, she ducked inside.

'Nick?' she called.

'Out the back.'

She walked through the reception area and out into his workshop. He had a Corvette up on the hydraulic lift and was standing in some kind of cement pit beneath it, fiddling with something on the underside of the car.

The car was a work of art.

So was Nick.

'Hey,' he said, shooting her a sidelong glance before turning back and concentrating on whatever it was he was doing. 'If it isn't the princess.'

'Hey, yourself, peasant.'

She glanced around the workshop. Light streamed in from the overhead lights, as well as from the large double doors that stood wide open, allowing her a glimpse of the yard and cottage opposite. It smelled of oil and grease, tools lay scattered about on benches, but beneath the chaos there was a definite order. Two cars were parked nearby, obviously awaiting his attention—a gleaming black Mercedes-Benz Pullman that had her eyes widening, and a 1970s Porsche 911 that had her mouth watering. He worked on the most amazing cars ever made, and yet he'd still taken the time to service her small sedan. It must have looked so out of place in here—a classic, girly hatchback in this... She swallowed. This was most definitely a *masculine* space.

Masculine...muscles...broad shoulders and strong thighs...arms that made a woman feel—

'Hey, princess, can you hand me that wrench there?'

Blair jumped. Heat flooded her cheeks. She stared wildly at the tool he pointed to, and then jerked forward and handed it to him.

He looked right at home, tinkering with that car...but she remembered him talking about his dream of running a nature retreat, the faraway look in his eyes when he'd mentioned it, and she wondered what had ever happened to that dream.

Life, she supposed. Life had got in the way.

'What are you doing?' She moved closer to see. Motor mechanic might not have been his first career choice, but his hands were swift and sure, his fingers strong, and she could tell he was good at what he did.

'Careful,' he warned as she moved closer again. 'I wouldn't want to ruin your party dress.'

That made her smile. She was wearing jeans, but her T-shirt was white, so she edged away again.

He hooked one of his devil-may-care grins in her direction and her lungs suddenly squeezed tight as the air in the workshop grew thick and heavy. 'You really shouldn't wear white, city girl.'

'Why not?' Her voice came out thready, breathy.

''Cos it makes me want to muss you up and get you dirty.'

This time when he hooked another of those grins at her his eyes lingered on her form in frank appreciation. Heat flared in her cheeks. When his gaze returned to her face his grin widened, as if he knew exactly what kind of reaction he was having on her.

He looked strong and lean and mean, with both

hands raised above his head unscrewing a bolt, and the fantasy hit her hard and fast. She could sashay down to him right now, hip-sway down those steps to join him in that pit—she could bring her seductive catwalk saunter into play—that would really make his eyes widen. She could stop in front of him, lean in close, touching at the thighs and the chest. She could reach up and push that lock of hair off his forehead and then lift her lips to his neck and close her mouth over the pulse beating wildly at the base of his throat, lave it with her tongue. And all the while his arms would be stuck in the air, holding onto whatever needed holding onto, and her lips could work their way up his jaw, nuzzling his day-old growth with a slowness that would make him start to shake the way he was shaking now. She'd work her way around to his mouth. Their lips would meet, their tongues would clash—

Nick gave a strangled curse.

Blair blinked…and then leapt back. *What was she doing?*

At exactly the same moment a jet of black liquid—thick and dirty—squirted from underneath the car and hit Nick full in the face.

Blair stared at him. He stared back, his arms still

raised above him. Kiss him? *Not now!* And then she started to shake with laughter. She suspected it was the sudden release in tension. Whatever it was, she couldn't stop herself literally howling. 'Oh, you should see your face, country boy!'

With an intent that she didn't at first recognise, he lowered his arms. 'You think that's funny, city girl?'

She held her sides as she doubled over. 'That's the funniest thing I've ever seen in, like, for ever!' she gasped out. 'It's beyond funny! Nicholas, you should've been a comedian. No, no.' She laughed harder. 'A clown at the circus. That was brilliant and—'

She broke off with a squeal when she found him advancing on her, purpose in his every step. She held a hand out to ward him off. 'Now, don't do anything hasty—something you might regret.'

'Oh, I'm not going to regret it, city girl.'

At that, she turned to run, but he grabbed her around the waist before she'd taken two steps, and with a swiftness that stole her breath he hauled her close and promptly wiped his face against her cheek.

'Brute!' she squealed, laughing harder as she tried to push him away. With absolutely no effect.

His arms were bands of steel and his chest a rock solid wall beneath her palms.

He grinned, and even through the oil and grease or whatever it was, that grin could still make her pulse stumble. 'Told you I wanted to mess you up, princess.'

'You…you guttersnipe!' she threw back, searching wildly for an appropriate insult as desire hit her hot and hard, pulsing with a life of its own.

He threw his head back and laughed at that. The action shot a streak of the black stuff from the tips of his hair to splatter across the front of her pristine white T-shirt. 'Look what you've done!' She tried to sound outraged.

'Hell, that was an accident. Honest.' But he was still grinning when he reached for a clean rag and made as if to blot it against the front of her shirt.

And then she remembered.

She froze.

Her laughter fled. *Oh, please, God, don't let him touch the prosthesis!* Her stomach filled with bile. 'Let me go, Nick.' The words croaked out of her.

'Lighten up, city girl. I—'

He broke off with a frown, staring down at her, his hand with the rag hovering over her chest but not touching her. Blair swallowed. Nobody had touched her prosthesis except her and her doctor. Shame gripped her. And fear and inadequacy.

She thrust against him. 'I said let me go!'

He loosened his grip, but his hands snaked up to curve around her upper arms, as if he sensed the strength had drained out of her. She pulled out of his grip to back up and sit on a stool before her legs gave out completely. No flip comment came to her aid, no easy or sophisticated banter. Just awkwardness, embarrassment.

And grief.

She closed her eyes, pain twisting her insides until she could barely breathe. That fantasy of kissing Nick, of sashaying over to him and pushing his control to the limits. That was all it was—a fantasy. Yeah, sure, they could generate the kind of heat that tempted them to tear at each other's clothes. But what about when he saw her naked? Passion would turn to disgust and pity, that was what. Like it had with Adam. She would never survive that same look reflected on Nick's face.

'Blair, are you okay? Are you feeling ill?' She heard him swallow. 'Did I hurt you?'

She had to open her eyes at that. 'No.' She shook her head.

'I'm sorry. I forgot.'

So had she. For a few glorious moments.

'I was just fooling around.'

She wanted to walk away, but her knees still felt too shaky to risk it. Nick upended a milk crate and planted himself in front of her, his eyes dark. 'If you're not feeling ill, and if I didn't hurt you, then what the hell just happened?'

'It's no big deal, Nicholas. Let's just forget about it.'

'Garbage! It's a huge deal if it makes you look like this.'

Her chin shot up. 'Like what?'

'As if you're going to faint. As if you're going to throw up!'

He splayed a hand through his hair, and even beneath the muck that covered his face she could see that he'd paled.

'Sorry,' he muttered. 'I didn't mean to snap. It's just…'

Oh, God, please don't let him say it!

'Hell, Blair, I thought I'd hurt you.'

And beneath all that muck she recognised sincerity.

She shook her head again, slowly this time. 'You didn't hurt me.'

'Then why…' he spread his hands '…*this*?'

She went to drop her face to her hands, but he grabbed her hands before she could and thrust the clean rag into them, gesturing to her face. She remembered then that her face was probably as dirty as his. She pretended to busy herself scrubbing her cheeks.

He didn't bother trying to clean himself up. He just sat there quietly, waiting.

She didn't know what to say. But it wasn't fair to let him think he was at fault.

'I…' She swallowed and cleared her throat. 'I thought you were going to…'

He frowned. 'To what?'

'I thought you were going to touch…*here*.' She gestured to her chest.

His skin turned grey. 'I wouldn't have intentionally hurt you for the world.'

'It wouldn't have hurt me.' She had to wipe that expression from his face. 'I…the scar is still a bit tender. If I knock myself or press the prosthesis against my chest a certain way it can make me wince.' Like when she'd tried to reach up to the top shelf of her wardrobe the other day and had fallen against it. 'But horsing around like we just were—that's fine.'

He surveyed her for a moment, his eyes dark. 'But…?'

She moistened suddenly dry lip. 'I haven't had anyone touch it. And I…' She swallowed. 'I thought you were going to, and…and I couldn't stand it.'

She hadn't thought he could possibly go any greyer, but he did. He didn't get up. He didn't say anything else.

'Look,' she suddenly blurted out. 'This is still something I'm adjusting to. I don't know what else you want me to say.'

'I want you to tell me how it made you feel.'

Her throat clenched. She had to swallow to loosen it. 'It made me feel awkward, embarrassed, vulnerable.' She had to swallow again. 'It made me feel ashamed and inadequate.'

His jaw dropped. 'Hell, Blair—'

'I know, I know.' She waved her hands in front of her face. 'My head tells me I have nothing to feel ashamed or inadequate about.'

'But?'

She wanted to close her eyes against the gentleness in his voice. 'But it's hard to make myself feel that.'

When she glanced up his eyes held hers, ordering her to finish her confession, compelling her to share it. 'Look, I'm a bit hung up about it.'

'Because?'

She stared down at her hands and found them twisting the rag convulsively. 'Because my boyfriend wasn't exactly a pillar of strength during my diagnosis.'

He stiffened. 'You have a boyfriend?'

'Had,' she corrected, and then found herself stifling a wry smile when his spine unbent again. 'The doctor showed us photographs of what my chest would look like after surgery and…um… he went running for the hills.'

Nick shot to his feet with an expletive that made her ears burn. 'What a jerk!'

'Yeah, that's what I thought. So I fired him.'

'Fired him?'

'Adam worked for me—was one of my designers.' She shrugged. 'He was a jerk. He was only using me to get ahead in the business. But I didn't see that until it was too late. I gave him his marching orders.' She leant back and folded her arms. Nick sat again. 'And, man, it felt good.'

Suddenly they were both laughing again, and Blair had no idea how it had happened. She was only grateful it had.

'Blair, I—'

'No, don't.' She didn't want him telling her how sorry he was. It would only make her feel heavy and shaky and defenceless again. 'I'm alive, and my prognosis is good. I have a lot to be grateful for.'

Those were the things she should be focussing on.

'And, speaking of things to be glad about, guess how many takers I have for my first class tomorrow?'

'Ten?'

'Higher.'

'Twelve?'

'Sixteen!'

He let out a whoop, his smile all she could have hoped for. 'That's brilliant. I told you you'd be in demand.'

'If I keep those numbers I'll make over eight hundred dollars for breast cancer research.'

'Keep those numbers? Heck, Blair, once word gets around those numbers will grow. I bet there'll be more than sixteen heads that show up tomorrow as it is.'

'More? I could make a thousand dollars—all for having some fun. How cool is that?' She straightened and smiled. 'That's why I dropped in. I wanted to thank you for coming up with the idea. I… It was a good idea.'

'Any time.'

But his attention was no longer on their conversation. His gaze had lowered to her lips and she knew he wanted to kiss her. An answering heat instantly surged through her.

She scrambled to her feet, wishing she could scatter her wayward desires to the four winds as easily. 'I…um…should get going. I'll see you on Sunday up at the school.'

'How about Stevie and I collect you at eleven?'

She shook her head and backed up as he rose too. He was just too big and broad, too tempting. 'No need. I'll make my own way there.'

And then she turned and made for the door.

'Hey, princess?'

She didn't break stride. 'What?'

'You might want to take the back exit. You look a mess.'

She changed direction. 'Go take a shower, peasant.' But she found she was grinning as she walked past him.

Nick saw Blair the moment she sauntered down to the school's sports field. Light grey cargo pants set the length of her legs off nicely. His hands itched to run up the lean length of those legs, to sample their sleek warmth and firm smoothness…to make her shiver with anticipation…to fire her with desire.

There were a hundred reasons why that was a no-go zone.

It didn't mean he could shake the thought from his head.

Gritting his teeth, he concentrated on laying out the softball diamond. And on not noticing who she spoke to or the admiring glances cast in her direction by the single guys and some not-so-single guys. That was hard, though. In her hot-pink T-shirt she stood out like some exotic bird. Muttering, he counted bats and balls.

When he next glanced in her direction—after he'd finished counting bats and balls—he found she'd moved closer to where he stood, and that she was surrounded by sixteen-year-old girls, all of whom obviously had a bad case of hero-worship.

He could relate to that.

She wore a scarf in her hair—hot pink and orange, with threads of gold that glittered in the sun. It held her hair back off her face. It looked bright and breezy, a touch flirty. He stumbled

sideways, nearly falling over a bat when he realised that the scarf wasn't for adornment. It was
an anchor to help keep her wig in place.

He swallowed. What if her wig came off in front
of all these people and—?

She lifted her hand and he suddenly realised she
was waving to him. 'Hey, city girl,' he called out,
filling his hands with bats and balls.

'First game is girls versus guys,' she called back.
'You're captain of the guys' team and I'm captain
of the girls'.' A cheer went up. 'And, believe me,
country boy, you guys are toast.'

He grinned as she and the girls went into a huddle, backsides wiggling as if to taunt every male
over the age of twelve. He'd lay money on a bet
that she and the girls had talked game tactics in
her class yesterday. Anticipation fired through
him. He couldn't wait for her to show him what
she had.

The girls gave a cheer and broke out of their
huddle. She jogged over to him.

'Heads or tails?' she demanded, with a delicious
lift of her eyebrows.

He remembered the way her backside had wig-
gled in that huddle. 'Tails.'

She tossed the coin. 'Heads!' she announced,

not even bothering to glance down at it, and she sent him such a cheeky grin that he realised exactly what kind of rules she had in mind—no rules. 'We're batting first, ladies!'

Another cheer went up and the game started.

The guys should have won, they really should, but the girls had used every low-down dirty trick in the book to trip the guys up…and it had worked. Nick had nearly choked when fifteen-year-old Paul Davidson was coming into the home plate for what should have been the winning run, and Stevie, Poppy, and Cheryl Smith called out, 'Paulie, hey, Paulie!' in sing-song unison, and had then lifted their shirts. Paulie had fallen flat on his face.

Out!

Beneath their shirts the girls wore tank tops with smiley faces printed on them.

'You witch!' he accused Blair when her team came up to shake hands.

'You boys were lucky to get a draw.'

'Ain't that the truth?' He groaned. 'But what are you teaching my daughter?'

'Why, the importance of winning at all costs, of course.'

The colour was high in her cheeks and her eyes

sparkled, and he'd never seen her looking more divine.

'Oh, that was the best fun I've had in ages.'

Him too, he suddenly realised.

'Blair, we're ready!'

'Oops, I'm up for skittles. You too?'

''Fraid not. I promised I'd get a softball game going for the younger kids.'

She glanced at the kids who'd started to group and mill behind him, and just for a moment her eyes dimmed. Was she thinking about the life it was no longer possible for her to have? His heart ached for her.

'Do you need a hand?'

'Maisey's helping me.' Maisey was a single mum who'd moved to the area a few years ago. Her five-year-old twins were the team captains for the game.

Blair blinked, her face suddenly smooth and unreadable. 'I'll catch you later, then.'

He didn't *catch* her for another hour and a half, when she came up to where he was manning the sausage sizzle. 'One?' he asked.

'Yes, please. With loads of onion.' Then she cocked her head to one side. 'Is this all you're going to do today—work?'

'The school was short of volunteers.' Besides, he didn't mind. He loved hanging out with the kids.

'Blair!' Maisey came racing up. 'It's the sack races. This is the best fun. I've saved you a sack.'

For a moment he imagined that panic flashed in Blair's eyes. When her hand made an unconscious movement towards her right breast he realised he hadn't imagined it at all. His gaze lowered to her chest. All that jumping. It might be awkward for her. Even painful.

'You *have* to take part, Blair. We're running a book. You're odds-on favourite.'

'No way!' Nick shot out from behind the barbecue plate and shoved a pair of tongs into Blair's hand. '*I'm* defending champion.' He pointed a finger at Blair's nose. 'Don't move from here until I get back. I mean to wipe the field with this one.' And with that he led Maisey away.

He didn't glance back to see if Blair was grateful or not.

He didn't glance back to see if she was relieved or…

Damn and blast! He didn't want to feel this kind of protectiveness for her, this tenderness.

His lips twisted. No, those things weren't the problem. It was the attraction that pounded at him

whenever she was near. The need to reach out and
touch her...kiss her.

And the sense of rightness that filled him when
they were together.

He had to fight it because it couldn't go anywhere. Blair had made that very clear. And him...?

At heart, Nicholas, you're a family man.

His hands clenched. The look on her face when
she'd told him how the cancer had affected her
fertility. He'd recognised the grief, the regret.

He heard her voice in his head—*Not your problem, country boy.* No, not his problem, but...

But nothing! He wiped the field by five lengths
in the sack races. When they announced that the
sprints were starting, he cleaned up in those too.

It wasn't until he emerged from the equipment
shed that Nick realised he wasn't the last one left
in the school grounds. Blair leant against the wall
a few feet from the door, bright and inviting in
her pink shirt and her colourful scarf, bright and
inviting in the afternoon sun.

'Hey,' she said.

'Hey yourself.' He hooked his thumbs into the
belt loops of his jeans. 'Is there something I can
do for you?'

He could see that his formality, his sudden distance, bothered her. He was sorry for it, but it was the way it had to be if he wanted to keep his sanity.

'Just wanted to check if you were done.'

'Why?'

'Because it's not what you can do for me, country boy, but what I can do for you.'

Images flooded him. He could think of a hundred things—

He did what he could to kill the images.

'I have a surprise for you.'

He remembered all the reasons he should stay away from her—she was vulnerable, she was leaving in three weeks…and there were the fertility issues she'd mentioned.

If—and it was a big if—he ever got serious with a woman again, they would have to fit perfectly. Physically he and Blair fitted just fine. In other areas…

'I…uh…I'm sorry, Blair, but I'm kind of tired.' The words croaked out of him.

Her eyes softened. 'No energy on your part will be required. And I promise that what I'm going to show you will blow your mind.'

She blew his mind.

She pushed away from the wall and squared up to him. 'Not scared, are you, country boy?'

'Never.'

'Then walk this way.'

Curiosity got the better of him. He locked the equipment shed and set off after her. Another hour or so of her company couldn't hurt. Then he'd start to work on his sanity and the distance.

She led him to her car. 'I'll drive,' he said automatically.

'Why?'

'Because I'm the guy.' And gentlemen drove ladies wherever it was they wanted to go.

'You said you were tired. Besides, I know where we're going.' She opened the passenger door and bowed low. 'Your chariot awaits.' She walked around to the driver's side. 'What?' she said when he continued to stand there. 'You want me to close the door after you too?'

He surrendered with a half-muttered exclamation.

'Relax, Nicholas,' she ordered, handing him a bottle of water. 'You've worked like a Trojan all day. No wonder you're tired. Take it easy, rehydrate, and let someone else do the work for a bit.'

He couldn't believe how good it felt to have

someone notice how much he'd done for the day. Not that he wanted thanks. It was just that someone had noticed and cared.

And now Blair wanted to look after him for a bit, and he found he wasn't anywhere near as averse to that idea as he should be.

Think about it later, he told himself. He would work out what it all meant then. He leant back against the headrest and waited to see where she'd take him.

CHAPTER EIGHT

NICK straightened when Blair turned off the main road leading up into the national park and onto a smaller gravel road. 'Where are we going?'

'You'll see.'

Her excitement and anticipation reached out and wrapped around him. It made him feel loose and easy, relaxed. One thing was for sure. Whatever she wanted to show him he was determined to enjoy it. She deserved that much.

She deserved a whole lot more than that.

He sent a sidelong glance in her direction and then turned in his seat to survey her more fully. She looked fresh and cool, even though she'd joined in a whole load of activities today. Her nose and cheeks were tinged with pink, as if she'd had a little too much sun, but it only served to highlight the clear purity of her skin and the blue of her eyes.

As if she sensed his gaze, she turned and briefly

met it, smiled as if she couldn't help it, before turning back to concentrate on the road.

It was becoming less of a road and more of a track.

'I think today I made great headway into proving my I'm-fit-and-healthy point.'

'I wouldn't argue with that.' He frowned. 'Though Glory wasn't there.'

'Ah, but lots of her friends were. Word will get around. She'll hear about it. I have no doubt about that.'

She sounded deliciously satisfied. And determined.

She slowed to negotiate a pothole. 'She'll be seventy in a couple of years, and while it's unlikely that I will ever convince her to slow down I can at least put her mind at rest about me.'

He sat up a bit higher. 'Are you worried about her health?'

She flashed him a smile. 'No. But I want her to be happy. And surely she'll be both happier and healthier if she's not worrying about me?'

Her smile shouldn't have the power to tighten his skin. But it did. He suddenly realised he felt as rested and revitalised as if he'd just had a solid eight hours of sleep.

Why?

Because he'd let her take over for a while? Or simply because he was with her?

She lifted a hand momentarily from the steering wheel to gesture towards the scenery. 'Isn't this glorious?'

It took him a moment to drag his gaze from her perfectly manicured nails, painted a sparkly pink, to gaze at the scenery that surrounded them. To his left rose a forest of tall eucalypts—mostly blue gums with their smooth white trunks and khaki-blue foliage, interspersed with ribbon gums and wattle trees. Come August the wattle would flower into golden glory and the blossoms would drench the air with their fragrance. To his right the land fell away in gentle rolling slopes, with the river glinting through the landscape here and there. In times of drought this would bleach to pale brown and white, but there had been a lot of rain in the last few years and the land looked lush and green…and as fresh and inviting as the woman sitting beside him.

'Here we are!'

He snapped to, suddenly realising he'd been staring at Blair again. He glanced out through the front windscreen…

And found himself staring at an old-style wooden homestead. A large homestead that oozed charm.

'I…um…' *This* was what she wanted to show him?

'This is the Forest Downs guesthouse.' She pushed out of the car and then leant down to add, 'It's up for sale.' She dangled what looked like a set of house keys at him.

She wanted to show him a guesthouse that was up for sale because…?

The nature retreat! He'd told her about his old castle-in-the-air dream of running a nature retreat. He swallowed and shifted on his seat, glanced up at the homestead. When he'd been younger he'd dreamed of running a place like this, of taking groups for guided hikes in the Barrington Tops National Park, of showing them the beauty and diversity of the flora and the fauna of the mountain range. He'd dreamed of hearty meals in a communal dining room, convivial conversation around a roaring fire with guests who felt like extended family. There had always been children, a lot of children. He'd planned it all down to the last detail.

He could still see it so vividly. But…

He'd given up on that dream.

He didn't budge from the car. For a moment his legs just wouldn't work. Blair couldn't give that dream back to him. It would be too impractical, too risky to pursue that kind of lifestyle change now. He was happy rebuilding classic cars and overseeing his other business interests.

He supposed he could add this property to his portfolio…

In the next instant he shook his head. This property could never be just a part of his portfolio—a money-making venture. It represented so much more.

It represented a way of life.

And forgotten dreams.

He couldn't drag his gaze from the homestead. Blair waited nearby. She didn't try to hurry him. It was as if she realised he needed time to think through the implications first. When he finally met her gaze, she raised the house keys. They swung back and forth from her fingers, and for a moment all he could see was Eve and the fruit of temptation.

'What's the verdict?' she called out. 'Shall we?'

He nearly fell out of the car in his haste. 'You bet!'

He might never dare resurrect that old dream, but he wanted to look inside that old homestead. *He had to.* Even if it was just to see what he was missing out on.

'Excellent.' She gave him the keys and let him lead the way.

The homestead boasted eight double bedrooms, all with French doors that led out to a wraparound veranda. The kitchen was industrial-sized, and both the communal living and dining rooms were generous and warm. At the back of the house the veranda extended to become a large deck. A huge wooden and cast-iron outdoor setting sat in pride of place. A barbecue stood to one side. This would be the perfect place to watch the sunset…to drink a beer on a hot summer's night…to toast marshmallows in winter.

The *perfect* place.

Blair gestured to one side, drawing his attention to a small cottage that huddled amid the trees. 'That's a three-bedroom caretaker's cottage.'

The cottage would be perfect for him and Stevie.

The thought slipped in under his guard and refused to leave.

She pointed to the land on the other side. 'The

council have approved plans for the building of four cabins along there.'

Which would be perfect for both guests and live-in staff.

He drank in the view. 'Why is the current owner selling?'

She leant down to rest her elbows on the deck railing. 'According to the real-estate agent he's moving to America.' She stared out at the view and drew a deep breath into her lungs. 'It must be a wrench leaving this place, though. The view is to die for, and the peace...'

With the afternoon sun casting long shadows and hazing the air blue, and with not even the slightest breeze sweeping through the trees, there wasn't any sound to break the stillness except the occasional birdcall. He leant down on the railing beside her to drink it all in. Then he stilled. Touching her arm, he held a finger up to his lips and then pointed to a family of wallabies that had come to feed on the grasses that bordered the lawn.

A soft sigh whispered out of her. 'Look—the mother has a joey.'

She was right. A small cheeky head with ears too long for its face peeped from its mother's pouch. With an inelegant roll it tumbled out, all awkward legs and long ears, to crop the grass in the shadow of its mother.

Blair gave a soft laugh. 'Those joeys are too cute for words. I bet this family is half tame.'

She could be right.

Moving slowly, so as not to startle them, she settled herself on one of the wide steps that led down to the lawn.

Nick stayed where he was. 'How long has the guesthouse been on the market?'

'Nearly a month.'

'Any interested parties?'

She glanced up at that, and searched his face. Her lips lifted. 'I'm thinking there might be.'

He laughed at that. The wallabies lifted their heads and stared at them. Then they went back to cropping the grass, evidently deciding Blair and Nick presented no threat.

'Why did you bring me here, Blair?'

She steepled her hands together and continued to stare out in front of her. Finally she turned. 'Life's too short to give up on your dreams, Nicholas. If there's one thing I've learned in the last few months it's that. We all of us put off doing those things that we really want to do, always thinking that there'll be time. But sometimes there is no time left. I think we should all be seizing life by the horns and living in the moment.'

If he lived in the moment he'd tumble her to the soft grass below and make love to her with all the intensity that stretched through his being. With an intensity that would prove to her how right they were for each other.

But then he remembered the way she'd frozen when she'd thought he might accidentally touch her prosthetic breast, and he knew that while she preached living in the moment she hadn't achieved that state herself yet.

A weight dropped to his shoulders. 'What are *your* dreams, Blair?'

Her eyes widened for a moment. Then she frowned. 'You know, I've been so focussed on getting through my treatment, getting well again… and concentrating on easing Glory's worry, that I haven't thought about that in some time.'

And she'd been busy grieving for dreams that could never now be. But she didn't say that out loud, and he had no intention of reminding her. So instead he said, 'Taking your fashion label to ever greater heights, maybe?'

He did a double-take when she grimaced.

'You know, I'm thinking maybe not. I haven't really wanted to admit this to myself, but it's become increasingly clear to me that the last few years haven't been all that satisfying. A lot of work and, yes, a lot of corresponding success...'

'But?'

Those clear baby blues turned to him, and he wanted to drown in them. He wanted to drown in them more than he'd wanted anything in his life.

'I've moved further and further away from the actual designing and more and more into management and promotion.'

He lowered himself to sit on the step beside her. 'So your success has led you away from the things about your job that you loved?'

'Exactly!' She propped her chin on her hands. 'I should hire a manager.'

'And move back into the design side of things again?'

'Maybe.'

He didn't like the fact that he wanted to press her for a definite decision. It was none of his business.

'You could always move back to Dungog and run deportment classes for teenage girls.' He'd meant the words to come out flip and jokey, but they emerged in deadly earnest.

Her head lifted. 'Glory would love it if I came home.'

Would *Blair* love it, though?

'I'd have to start calling you a bumpkin.' This time he managed to be jokey.

'Doesn't have quite the same ring as princess.'

'Guess not.' But as she shifted on her step, tucking one long leg beneath her and leaning back against the railing, he knew that in his mind she'd always be a princess.

'I'll have to give my future some thought. What we're supposed to be talking about, however, is *your* future, Nicholas.'

'Why?'

'That's what all this is about.' She gestured to the homestead and the surrounding property. 'Why aren't you going after your dreams?'

'I gave this one up a long time ago.'

She shrugged. An elegant lift of one shoulder. 'You could resurrect this particular dream if it meant enough to you. But I'm not just talking about the nature retreat. I'm talking about children—your children. The children you want.'

His mouth soured. Even if Blair did stay in town, the fact of the matter was that children did not figure in her future.

'Maisey has a crush on you. Why don't you ask her out?'

'Heck, Blair!' Every muscled tightened in protest. 'She's a vegan who burns incense and drives a motorised scooter.'

'And she loves kids.'

'While I'm a dyed-in-the-wool carnivore who smells of engine oil and loves V8 engines.'

'And you also love kids.'

He couldn't think of a single thing to say. Blair had kissed him the way she'd kissed him… and now she wanted to set him up with another woman?

He was a Grade A idiot! Their kiss hadn't meant anything to her. Just because he might be interested in pursuing something more than a holiday fling it didn't mean she was.

He scrubbed a hand down his face. What the hell…? He *wasn't* interested in anything more than a fling.

He wasn't even interested in a fling!

His mouth suddenly dried.

'You're nit-picking, Nicholas. Maisey has a good heart. She's young and pretty, and—'

'We dated a while back. It didn't work out.' *He couldn't want more than a fling with Blair because...*

Blair folded her arms. 'That's hardly surprising when you're so busy finding fault with her and focussing on the negatives.'

'Look, I tried to focus on the positives. I wish I could fall in love with her.' He really did. Life would be *so* much simpler if he was in love with Maisey. 'But...'

She stared. 'But what?'

'She doesn't ring my bell, if you get my drift.' He enunciated the words carefully, to make sure she did get his drift. The fact of the matter was that Maisey didn't do it for him. But Blair sure as hell did. From the sudden heightening of colour in her cheeks he figured that she did take his meaning.

'What about Lisa Hodge? The real-estate agent?'

'We have different political affiliations. Very different. All we'd do is fight.'

'Fine! Well, then, how about—?'

He leapt to his feet. 'Enough, already! You can't

just pick out a woman for me and make it work. That's not how it's done.'

She leapt to her feet too. The wallabies bolted. 'Well, sitting on your backside and letting the grass grow around you isn't how it's done either!' She lifted her chin and slammed her hands to her hips.

He stabbed a finger at her nose. 'I messed up big time with Sonya. I'm not messing up again. If I ever take the plunge into matrimony again I'm going to get it right.'

She gave a seriously unsophisticated snort. 'You're so scared of getting it wrong that you won't settle for any woman. And you know why? Because you're waiting for Ms Perfect, that's why, and Ms Perfect doesn't exist. And you want to know something else, buster? You're not exactly Mr Perfect yourself!'

It hit him then. He had messed up again. Bigtime. He didn't understand what it meant, or the deeper implications, only that he was no longer prepared to meekly walk away from this woman.

And he had no intention of making it easy for her to walk away from him either. They had chemistry, he and Blair, but they had something more too. Rapport. An affinity that, if nurtured, had the potential to develop into something deep and unique. If only they dared to take the chance to explore it.

And he, for one, was tired of running.

Blair hated the relief that fizzed through her at Nick's complete lack of interest in Maisey. Or in any other woman for that matter. It made her angry—which was why she'd told him off so roundly.

She didn't want him for herself, so the relief was—

Yes, you do.

The words whispered through her. She stilled. She swung away to worry at her thumbnail. Yes, she did. She wanted Nick all to herself. What was the point in lying about it? Nick could heat her blood with one dark glance and have her mind racing to supply heavenly erotic images before he'd even touched her.

But then she'd remember her maimed body and the desire would rush back out of her with a speed that could leave her vaguely nauseous.

Okay, she wanted Nick. But that didn't mean they had a future together. If they'd met before her breast cancer…

She bit her thumbnail down to the quick. A future—a romantic future—was out of the question, and the sooner Nick was off-limits the better.

He'd be off-limits if he had a girlfriend.

He'd be off-limits if he had a wife and babies.

The image filled her mouth with so much bile she found it hard to swallow.

'You have no right to preach to other people, Blair!'

She swung back at the anger in his voice. His face was distorted with emotion, and it reminded her of their very first meeting when he'd let rip at her.

'You're not exactly Ms Hospital Corners, are you?'

What on earth...? 'What are you talking about? I said I needed to reassess my life, my future. It's not something I'm going to let slide, believe me.' Not after all she'd been through.

'Then start being honest. If not with me then at least with yourself. Stop lying to yourself.'

He moved in close, crowding her space, filling her with his hot, heady scent. She refused to give way. Pride kept her chin high. 'What are you talking about, country boy?' Her attempt to lighten the mood didn't work. Nick's eyes didn't soften with humour. They remained hard and bright with purpose.

'Until you accept yourself, Blair, the way you are now, until you stop feeling ashamed of the way your body looks, you're never going to find peace—and you sure as hell won't find happiness.'

His words sliced at her like knives. 'Ashamed of my body?' Her voice rose. 'I'm grateful to it for being strong enough to cope with the surgery and the treatment. I—'

'And that's another thing! What the hell is that all about? All this talk about being glad and grateful for what you have? You're human, aren't you? You're allowed to be angry that you've lost a breast. You're allowed to be furious that it's affected your fertility. Hell, Blair, you're allowed to *grieve*!'

His words slammed into her and she found herself giving way, stepping back. She found herself wanting to flee into the forest, to follow the same path as the wallabies and to run and run until she was too tired to feel any more.

She spun on Nick instead. 'Don't tell me how I should and shouldn't feel! What on earth do *you* know about it? You've never had cancer. You don't know what it's like to look in a mirror and not recognise yourself. You don't know what it's like to see the shock in a loved one's face as they watch the physical change in you—when they walk past your hospital bed because they haven't recognised you and it's only been a day since their last visit.'

Nick paled. 'Blair, I'm—'

'No.' She didn't want to hear his apology. 'You tell me I'm allowed to grieve and get angry? Don't you think I've done those things? You don't have a clue!'

'Then tell me.'

The weariness she'd craved hit her now. Problem was, she couldn't sink into oblivion.

'Tell me how you're really feeling, Blair.'

'I'm feeling a million things.' All at once. And it was starting to take its toll. She sank back down to the step, threaded her arm through the railing, and leant her head against it.

'Tell me just one.' He sat down too. Not touching her, mindful of her space, but close enough if she showed any sign of wanting physical contact.

She stared at the spot where the wallabies had grazed. 'Scared,' she finally said. 'Scared that without warning, the cancer will come back. Scared that I'll have to go through all that treatment again. Or, worse, that treatment won't be an option. I'm not ready to die.'

To his credit, Nick didn't try to reason that fear away with talk about today's medical break-throughs and about doctors monitoring her so closely that her chances of a full recovery were good. It was as if he sensed she knew all those things already. It was just that sometimes in the cold hours of dark those things couldn't help her rationalise her fear away.

'I'm scared that my life will never feel normal again. I'm scared that from here on fear will rule my life. And anger. And grief.'

'And that's why you've been trying to focus on the positives?' he finally said. 'That's why you keep reminding yourself of all the things you have to be grateful for.'

He did get it. 'Yes.' She met his gaze. 'You think that's wrong?'

He shook his head. 'Sounds smart to me.'

They were both silent for a bit. Nick cleared his throat. 'Have dinner with me.'

The change in topic threw her. 'I…'

'Not as friends,' he said, his voice growing stronger. 'I'm asking you out on a date.'

Her jaw dropped. She'd thought they'd sorted this out. 'Why?'

'Because I like you. I like you a lot. I want to kiss you again. I always want to kiss you. I want to see where it—us—could go, see what it could develop into.'

His words, particularly the ones about kissing, dissolved her listlessness in a microsecond. 'No!'

'Why not?'

'Nicholas, I'm going back to Sydney in a couple of weeks.'

'So? It's not the end of the earth. We could continue to see each other. Perhaps not as much as we'd like, but we'd sort something out. If things became serious I could move to the city or you could move back here.'

'No!' She shot to her feet, trembling all over. 'I am *not* the right woman for you.'

He rose to his feet a lot more slowly, his eyes taking every bit as much time in their appraisal of her. His hot brown gaze travelled from her feet all the way up her legs to her hips and torso, and then to her shoulders and chin until they met her gaze, appreciation rife in his eyes. It made her tremble.

'Now, why would you say that, I wonder?'

His words, his gaze, taunted her with everything

she could no longer have. Her pulse went mad at the lopsided grin he sent her and the knowing glint in his eye. 'You want children,' she choked out. 'I can't have them. How's that for starters?'

'Not bad,' he admitted. 'But, like I said before, there are other avenues.'

'None of which I'm prepared to pursue.' She swallowed. What would he say if he ever found out that it was fear that held her back from pursuing those other options? He would loathe her.

'That's something we'd need to negotiate down the track if things became serious.'

His soft words clogged her throat with fear, but beneath the fear a thread of excitement nudged through her. She shook her head, determined to ignore it. 'No.'

'Yes.' He planted his feet, held his ground.

'I'm not ready for a relationship! I need time.'

'I'm happy to give you all the time you need, Blair. I'm not asking you to jump immediately into bed with me. Nor am I asking you to marry me. I'm asking you to dinner. I'll pick you up, we'll go somewhere nice to eat, maybe dance. I'll drive you home, walk you to your door, and kiss you good-night.'

The scenario he painted was so vivid she could picture it.

'And then I'll go home.'

Yearning swamped her…and for a moment, hope. Nick made it all sound so easy and reasonable. And then the look of horror on Adam's face rose up through her and blocked everything else out. She took a step away from him. 'Thank you for the kind invitation, Nicholas, but no.'

Before he'd charged off into the sunset Adam had told her that men were visual creatures.

Visual?

Undoubtedly.

Creatures?

Beasts, more like.

Nick took two steps towards her until their bodies all but touched. His heat beat at her. 'You say you don't want fear ruling your life? Sometimes you have to face your fear head-on.'

She shook her head. 'I need time.'

The gold in his eyes flashed fire. 'Sometimes time isn't what you need. Sometimes what you need is a push. What Adam did, Blair, was terrible—unforgivable. But most men would never act like that.'

She didn't want to believe Nick would act

like that. Everything inside her protested at the thought. But…

'Until you risk another Adam moment the fear will continue to grow. So have dinner with me and don't let the fear win.'

He might be right. But he could be wrong. And she wasn't going to risk it. Not yet. Maybe when the memory of Adam's betrayal grew fainter. But until then…

She stepped back and shook her head. 'No.'

Nick stared at her, the lines around his eyes becoming more pronounced, the lines around his mouth turning white. She almost relented at the disappointment that scored his eyes. She swallowed the impulse down. This was for the best.

He folded his arms. 'I won't give up.'

Panic threatened to rise in her then. 'You have no right to lecture or to push me! For the last twelve years you've done whatever you can to avoid any real commitment.'

'But I'm not now.'

'What's to say you won't turn and run like the wind if I change my mind?'

His eyes gleamed. 'Why don't we put that to the test? Say you'll have dinner with me.'

'No.'

She didn't dare. She didn't have the resources to cope with a rejection from Nick, no matter how nicely he phrased it. Maybe he wouldn't reject her. Maybe he would be able to cope with her scar, her lack of a breast. But her judgement had let her down once in Adam. She no longer trusted it. And she didn't have any courage left.

He opened his mouth but she cut him off. 'Are we done here?' She pointed to the guesthouse.

'For the moment.'

She didn't know if he referred to the property or their conversation, and she didn't ask.

They drove back to Dungog in silence.

CHAPTER NINE

BLAIR took a deep breath, and then, lifting her chin, opened the gate and breezed into Nick's backyard. The huge double doors of the workshop stood wide open and she could see Nick working inside.

She wondered what it was about a man in overalls carrying a wrench in his back pocket and a grease gun in his hands that could instantly soften a woman's belly and turn her knees to water.

He just looked…so capable.

He'd be good with his hands.

Her cheeks heated up at the thought. Nick chose that moment to turn. He shaded his eyes against the early-afternoon light and then stilled. Without haste, he wiped his hands on a rag and then sauntered out to meet her.

'Hello, Blair.'

Blair. Not city girl or princess.

'Hello, Nicholas.'

'What can I do for you?'

She hated his formality and she had no intention of following suit. 'Ah—it's not what you can do for me, but what I can do for you. I come bearing lunch.' She lifted the two brown paper bags she carried, imprinted with the logo of the bakery opposite Nick's workshop. 'You *do* know that these pies have a state-wide reputation?'

'With some reason.'

She gestured to his outdoor seating. 'Do you have time to join me?'

He adjusted his stance. With his legs spread wide and one hand on his hip, he made her mouth water. 'Is this a lunch *date*, Blair?'

'No!' The word shot out of her. 'I mean…it's just lunch between friends.'

'Then I'm sorry. But I'm afraid I'm busy.'

She refused to let his attitude defeat her. 'I've come with a business proposition. But before I put that to you I wanted to check and make sure that you were keeping up your end of our bargain.'

His other hand went to his hip too. 'What bargain?'

She lifted the brown paper bags again, and with a raised eyebrow glanced pointedly at his outdoor furniture. She'd seen grown men almost weep at the scent of these pies, but Nick seemed strangely immune.

'You have fifteen minutes,' he said with an unflattering bluntness.

He disappeared back into the workshop. Blair settled herself at the table. He emerged a couple of minutes later, hands washed and carrying two cans of soda.

'What deal?' he said again, setting one can in front of her and taking the seat opposite. He accepted the paper bag she slid across to him.

'The one where you agreed to take care of Stevie's fundraising efforts.'

For a moment she thought he might smile. He didn't, and that was when it hit her—that was what had been missing from the moment he had turned and found her in his yard. He hadn't smiled. Not once.

She promptly lost her appetite. She opened her can of soda to hide her sudden bewilderment. To hide how he rattled her.

'Of course I'm keeping up my end of the bargain.'

'What are you doing?'

He leant back in his seat, pie untouched, and folded his arms. This time he did smile, and it made her heart strut about in her chest as if it was on a catwalk. 'You led me to believe that the role of fundraising manager would be difficult, time consuming, and onerous.'

She forced her eyes wide. 'I did no such thing. I didn't tell you what it would involve at all.'

'But you knew what I thought…and you let me believe it.'

She made her eyes even wider. 'The only thing I might have *perhaps* misled you about was the fact that I wouldn't help Stevie unless you agreed to get involved. I was always going to help Stevie.'

'So your blackmail was…?'

'A bluff,' she agreed.

He shook his head. 'Of course it was.'

'I figured you deserved it after you'd abused me so abominably.'

He shifted uncomfortably. 'I'd already apologised for that.'

Regret gleamed in the depths of his eyes. Her drink halted halfway to her mouth. 'It is okay, Nicholas. We sorted it.'

'So that's not the reason you won't have dinner with me?'

Soda shot up her nose as she took a sip. She grabbed a paper napkin to mop her face. 'What?'

'Because of my temper?'

'No! I told you—it's me, not you. I'm just not ready.'

His eyes grew opaque. She wished with all her heart that he'd call her city girl, or princess, that he'd tease her.

He continued to ignore his pie. 'I think that's just an excuse you're hiding behind.'

She pushed her can of drink away. 'We've already had this discussion.'

'Then what are you doing here, Blair?'

She clenched her jaw and told herself he was only trying to get a rise out of her.

He made a show of slapping a hand to his forehead. 'That's right—you wanted to talk fundraising!'

She refused to fall for it. 'As I am no longer the official Miss Showgirl mentor, I wanted to offer my services to Stevie. I'm sure I can come up with something fabulous for the auction.'

That made him still. 'You mean it?'

'Of course I mean it.'

'Why Stevie?'

'Because she was the one who first made me realise that I might actually have something useful to offer.'

And through Stevie she'd met Nick. And Nick was the first person who'd treated her as if she was normal. Around Nick she always felt normal.

He frowned. 'As far as I can tell, all this fund-raising gig involves is helping Stevie sell the endless bars of chocolate she seems to have access to.'

'Chocolate for charity,' she clarified.

'And there's some kind of gala dinner associated with that auction you just mentioned.'

'That just about sums it up.'

'Nothing else?'

'Nope. The girls are in charge of decorating the hall and catering for the dinner. The money raised from the tickets for the dinner will be divided among the girls equally. It's their individual offerings for the auction, though, that go towards their individual tally. This is where parents and friends can get involved.'

'I thought I could put a car service up for grabs.'

'That's an excellent idea.' It shouldn't surprise her that he'd given it some thought.

'And Stevie is going to offer herself as a girl Friday for a month to the local businesses in the area.'

'It'll be good work experience for her too.'

'I wasn't sure what else to do or how much more I should be doing.'

She hesitated.

'Spill,' he ordered.

'I'm not saying you *should* do this, mind, but there are a lot of people—older folk—who'd love to bid…and win…but who can't afford the more expensive things like a car service. Also…' She glanced up at him and found him watching her closely. Her heart surged against her ribs.

'Also?'

She cleared her throat. 'Also it could be kind of nice if you and Stevie did something together.'

'Like?'

'Like washing cars, maybe. Or something like that,' she added quickly. 'I was just thinking mechanic…cars…et cetera.'

He leant back. 'That's a nice idea. I'll run it by Stevie—and Poppy too. Thanks.'

She suddenly felt self-conscious under his too-penetrating scrutiny.

'Blair, if you really want to help…'

She leant forward. 'Yes?'

'It'd be kind if you could take Poppy under your wing. Her mother is finding things a bit tough at the moment, and can't really help out much. She's baking a cake for the auction, and Poppy is going to put her babysitting services up for auction, and I've assured her that's all fine, but…'

He didn't need to spell it out. Poppy would feel second-rate compared to the other girls. Given Poppy's self-consciousness, Blair admired her all the more for pushing herself to take part in the quest. 'She's practically another member of your family, isn't she?'

'She and Stevie have been friends since kindergarten.' He shrugged. 'This is practically Poppy's second home.'

She stared at him and knew she'd been right not to have dinner with him. Nick was a born father, and he deserved more kids. Lots more kids. Her heart burned and her stomach churned, as if in rebellion at her conclusion, but she knew she was right.

Ha! It's not as if you're making some noble sacrifice, she derided herself. She hadn't lied to Nick. She wasn't ready for any kind of romantic entanglement. Regardless of how slow he promised they'd take it. When they kissed, neither one of them could remember the meaning of the word *slow*.

Problem was, she could suddenly and vividly

imagine falling into a sensual embrace and making love with Nick.

Her breath caught. Her pulse raced. She swallowed and pulled back. Shut off the images. That meant risking more than she was prepared to. She couldn't go there. She *wouldn't* go there.

'Eat up, Blair.' Nick nodded towards the paper bag that held her pie. His remained untouched. 'It'll get cold. Besides, your fifteen minutes is nearly up.'

He was serious!

'But you can rest assured,' he continued, 'that I'm keeping up my end of our bargain.'

'Don't you take longer than fifteen minutes for lunch?'

'For lunch *dates* I do. But rarely for impromptu business lunches.'

She didn't reach for her pie. If she tried to eat it now she had a feeling it might just choke her. 'Are you going to stay mad at me for ever for turning down your dinner invitation?'

Unlike her, he finally reached for his pie and pulled it from its paper bag. The scent hit her, making her stomach tighten. He bit into it as if to delay his answer, as if to make her wait. She watched the way his mouth closed around the golden pastry, the way a flake stuck to the corner of his mouth and how his tongue reached for it, and she had to wrench her gaze away.

'I'm not angry with you, Blair. I'm just pulling back, withdrawing—like you obviously want me to.'

But she *didn't* want him to! They could still be friends, couldn't they?

She ignored her pie to fold her arms. She knew exactly how to get him to *un*-withdraw. 'Fundraising was only one of the issues I wanted to discuss with you today. As time is obviously of the essence, I'll get to the crux of my business proposition without further ado. Nicholas, if I bought the Forest Downs guesthouse, would you consider investing in it with me?'

She wanted him to follow his dream. She wanted him to remain her friend. And she wanted him off-limits romantically. It might be possible to achieve all those things in one fell swoop.

He didn't blink. He didn't still. He didn't fire up with instant enthusiasm. He didn't do any of the things she'd expected…or hoped. He just sat there and calmly ate the rest of his pie.

'I'd be a silent partner. You'd be free to run it however you wanted.'

Finally he wiped his fingers on a napkin and sat back.

'Well?' It took a superhuman effort not to shout the question at him.

'Why would you make me that kind of offer?'

At least this was a question she'd expected. And she'd rehearsed her answer. 'The guesthouse is in a beautiful location—a beautiful part of the world that I think other people should have the chance to experience. I think you could turn that guesthouse into something special. You have vision. You'd promote environmental awareness and tourism, both at the same time. You'd help to create interest and awareness for the endangered species that call the national park home while bringing tourism dollars into the area. It seems…a worthwhile thing to do.'

'And what would *you* get—other than a warm, fuzzy feeling?'

She frowned at the mockery in his voice. This wasn't how she'd expected this to go. 'Obviously I'd expect profits down the track. The other advantage, of course, is that I'd almost always be guaranteed a room whenever I came to stay.'

'You don't think I can afford to buy the guesthouse on my own, do you?'

'Actually, I know you could afford to buy it out-right if you wanted. I checked your business pro-file on the internet. Your net worth is more than mine, and I'm not crying poor. Blair Mac Designs was doing very well.'

'Prying, Blair?'

'Not really. I didn't want to show you the guest-house if you couldn't afford to move on it. That would've been cruel. But I've got to ask… How on earth have you managed to build up such an attractive property portfolio in just ten years? And yes,' she added before he could open his mouth, 'now I *am* prying.'

For a moment she thought he might smile. She wanted him to smile. Just how badly shocked her. He didn't.

'I completed a business degree by distance learning after Sonya died. And I studied the stock market. Closely.'

He must have an amazingly shrewd brain in that gorgeous head of his. She pursed her lips, glanced around. 'And yet you work when you don't have to, and you certainly don't live the high life.'

'Stevie and I have everything we need.'

It hit her then. Nick had made sure that money, or more accurately the lack of it, could never adversely affect him and his again. He'd made sure that he could provide for *all* his family, each and every member, if the need ever arose.

She wanted to reach out and touch him, to tell him he didn't always have to be the strong one. But unless she was prepared to let their relationship evolve to the next step she didn't have that right.

And she balked from taking that next step.

She shook herself. 'So—the guesthouse. I could afford to buy it outright myself, but I don't want to run it.'

'What *do* you want?'

'I want a base in the area.' Returning home to Dungog held a lot of appeal, but she couldn't just up sticks from Sydney on a whim. She needed a plan. She needed to make sure her manager in Sydney was up for the job before she returned home for good.

'What kind of split were you looking at? Fifty-fifty? Or more like sixty-forty or seventy-thirty your way?'

'I hadn't thought that far. But I'd be happy to be the majority stakeholder.'

He laughed, but he didn't smile. 'So...you'd be the boss. Therefore if I did anything wrong, if I did something you didn't like, you'd try to buy me out. In effect fire me. Just like you fired Adam, right?'

Her jaw dropped. 'This is nothing like that! This has nothing to do with Adam.'

'On the contrary, I think it has everything to do with him.'

'This is purely business! Adam and I made the mistake of mixing business with the personal. You and I know better than that.'

'Forget it.' He speared a finger down onto the table between them. 'I *want* the personal. What's more, I think you do too, and it frightens you so much that you're looking for ways to create an artificial distance between us. I'm not going to be a party to that.'

Her jaw went slack. She tried to stiffen it.

'Sorry, Blair.' He rose. 'Lunchtime is over.'

She sat there and watched him walk away, and then she shot to her feet too. 'What? So we can't even be friends?'

He stilled. Then he turned. His face had gone grey. His eyes had lost their glitter. Her heart leapt into her throat, making it impossible to speak.

'I've told you what I want, Blair.'

A romantic relationship? She couldn't do it.

'I'm not a masochist. I'll always want more than you're prepared to give. So, no, we're not going to be friends.'

'You said you'd give me time!' She didn't know where that plea came from. She only knew it was real.

'And you told me not to bother—that there was no hope you'd change your mind.' He shifted his stance. 'Are you saying it has changed?'

She wanted to say yes. She opened her mouth… She closed it again and shook her head.

'Then, for my own protection, I'm pulling back.'

He didn't try to hide his disappointment from her, or his pain, and it beat at her like a living, breathing thing. Her eyes stung. She swallowed back a lump.

'I'm sorry.'

He smiled one of those crooked smiles. 'Now, *that* I do believe.' His face softened. 'I hope you find whatever it is you need to make you happy, Blair.'

She'd have said the same back to him but her throat had closed over entirely. It all sounded so final!

And when he turned and strode back into the interior of his workshop without once glancing behind him she knew there was a reason it felt so final.

Because it was.

Barely able to see, she stumbled out of the yard and made her way back home. She let herself in at the gate, dropped to her knees in front of one of Glory's flowerbeds and started pulling weeds.

CHAPTER TEN

'STOP fussing, Aunt Glory.' Blair batted her aunt's hands away from where they fidgetted with the hem of her shirt. 'You look fabulous.'

She and Glory stood in line in the foyer of the town hall for the Miss Showgirl gala dinner, and Glory did indeed look stunning. She wore a pair of wide silk trousers—black—and a stunning cobalt blue blouse encrusted with crystals. Blair had whipped up the outfit during the week.

Glory's garden kept her busy during the day. Making this outfit for her aunt had kept her busy during the evenings. Evenings where she'd been careful to shun all make-up and her wig after her nightly shower. Evenings spent in PJs, just like the old days. Evenings when she did her best to seem like her old self in the hope that an assumed nonchalance about her appearance would help Glory relax.

She blew out a breath. Hopefully the item she'd

put up for tonight's auction would keep her busy this coming week.

Glory touched her blouse. 'This is the most beautiful outfit, Blair. I can't seem to stop touching it, playing with it. I'm going to be the envy of the co-operative crowd, not to mention the women on the show committee.'

It hit Blair then that she hadn't made an outfit for her aunt in years. Once upon a time...

'I have to say it did my heart good to see you bent over your sewing machine this week.'

'It did mine good too,' Blair admitted. 'In the last few years work has become so busy that I seem to spend less and less time actually designing and making clothes, and more time on management and marketing.'

Glory glanced up, her eyes suddenly shrewd. 'I thought you enjoyed it?'

'I did. I do.'

'But?'

'But I don't love it the way I love making beautiful clothes.'

'Of course not. That's the price of success, though, dear.'

They reached the front of the line and handed their tickets over. As she followed Glory into the grand ballroom she said, 'So you don't think that's fickle of me?'

'Acknowledging your first love? No, of course not. After everything you've been through I'd be surprised if you weren't re-evaluating and reassessing.'

Blair stopped, pulled her aunt to a halt. 'So you know that's what I've been doing?'

'Of course.'

Glory knew her too well. 'And do you know what conclusion I've come to?'

'I don't think you have yet.'

'But...' Blair moistened suddenly dry lips. 'But if I decided to return home to Dungog you wouldn't mind?'

'I'd love it.'

'I wouldn't cramp your style?'

'I have no style to cramp.'

Suddenly both Blair and Glory were laughing. Blair seized two glasses of champagne from the tray of a passing waiter and handed one to her aunt.

'You're drawing the eye of every man in the room,' Glory observed as they sipped their champagne.

The observation didn't make Blair flinch as it

would have three weeks ago, when she'd first arrived back in town. Coming home had been good for her. It had been good for Glory too.

Then she caught sight of Nick in a tuxedo, and her heart gave one huge thump and the bubbles of champagne worked their way into her bloodstream. It took a moment to catch her breath.

Glory followed her gaze. 'He's a good-looking man.'

And he was certainly busy checking her out! Even from across the room she could feel the burning heat of his appraisal. His hunger made her swallow. She did what she could to submerge the answering hunger that surged through her.

She turned her back, suddenly aware that she'd worn this red silk dress—a deceptively demure wraparound that revealed a startling amount of thigh when she walked—for Nick's benefit. And for Nick's benefit alone. She bit her lip in consternation.

'Nick Conway is smokin' hot,' she hammed, fanning her face. 'He's also utterly infuriating.'

Glory chuckled. 'Sounds promising, then.'

'Don't you believe it,' she returned wryly. 'I do know one thing for sure, though.'

'What's that?'

'We can't let all this attention go to waste. Follow me.'

Nick tried to pick his jaw up from the floor. He brushed one hand across his chin to make sure he wasn't drooling.

Blair looked stunning!

He shook his head in an attempt to clear it. As far as he was concerned she always looked stunning, but tonight…

Tonight she was something else—a golden siren dressed in red—and it drew his skin tight across his frame, made his muscles tense and twitch and his mouth dry with a burning, blazing need.

He ran a finger around the collar of his dress shirt and ordered himself to look away, but his eyes refused to obey the command. They refused to do anything but devour her where she stood.

When their eyes had met she hadn't smiled hello. She'd turned her back. That was his fault. Because of the way he'd dismissed her through the week. But it hadn't stopped his heart from slumping. Damn it! He was supposed to be keeping his distance, pulling back, withdrawing. Blair turning away should help him do the same. Except…

She'd flashed a gorgeous length of golden thigh at him as she'd turned and it had taunted him, teased him. It held him captive. Even now.

She shifted her weight and the curve of her backside beneath the thin red silk snared his attention. All he could think about was how it would feel if he pulled that delectable curve against his groin and bent his mouth to touch his lips to the sensitive skin behind her ear.

Her clear laugh and Glory's deeper one hauled him back. *She's off-limits!* But as she and her aunt moved to the table displaying many of the wares up for auction this evening rather than backing off and moving away he found himself drawing closer to the table too. He didn't like the way Ben Pengally was eyeing Blair, as if trying to memorise the length of her legs. Or the way Graham Bourke was touching her on the arm to claim her attention.

His hands clenched. His teeth ground together. Every man in the room was watching her, either overtly or covertly, as if they wanted a piece of her. Furthermore, she was doing nothing to discourage it.

'Oh, Aunt Glory, that cake!'

Her voice was clear enough to travel along the

length of the table and beyond. Nick glanced at the cake. It looked pretty good, but as far as he could tell it was just a cake. Nothing to go into raptures over.

'Poppy's mother made it, and she's an absolute marvel,' Blair continued. 'It's a proper German *sachertorte*. I hope whoever wins it invites me to their table for dessert.'

Nick swore that every man in hearing distance swung to stare at the cake.

He slammed his hands to his hips. It took every ounce of strength he possessed not to stride over there, kiss her senseless and claim her for his own. He'd been an idiot to back off so soon. He dragged a hand through his hair. He'd told her he wouldn't give up, but he had. At the very first roadblock. Pathetic!

He thrust out his jaw. If she was having dessert with anyone tonight it would be with him.

The MC asked the crowd to take their seats. Nick resisted the urge to kick his chair. Why hadn't he organised to share a table with Blair and Glory?

His frustration lowered a couple of notches when he realised her table consisted mostly of the co-operative staff. It ratcheted up again a moment later, though, when he turned to find her laughing at something Ethan Craig was saying, and when she answered a hearty wave from Andrew Logan with a big smile and a mouthed hello.

She was flirting!

She'd told him she wasn't ready for anything romantic and he'd believed her. He remembered the way she'd fired to life in his arms and his hands clenched. He called himself every kind of fool he could think of.

Blair was a butterfly emerging from her cocoon and testing her wings. Rough handling would bruise her, wound her. He shifted on his chair. Beneath the table his foot tapped. If Blair was ready to start dating again, then he was going to be the first in line. He would be gentle with her, tender. He would make her laugh. He would make her feel beautiful. He would make her want him, desire him.

He would force her to acknowledge his potential as a mate.

And much, much more.

He turned as someone took the seat beside him. 'Hiya, Nick. This is going to be fun, isn't it?'

Maisey. He forced a smile from uncooperative lips. 'Absolutely.'

Maisey cheerfully chattered on, but Nick only heard every other word. Sandalwood and the scent of incense swamped him, making him sneeze. And then he had a brainwave. 'Can you excuse me for a moment, Maisey?'

He leapt up and made his way to one of the auction's organisers. 'Can I add another item to the list?' His smile broadened as the organiser took down all the details. Blair wouldn't be able to resist.

The auction took place between courses. Where possible, the contributor was asked up to the microphone to give a sales pitch. The bidding was often fast and furious, and Nick would have enjoyed it if he hadn't been so focussed on the woman two tables over.

Soon it was his turn to stride up to the microphone and start the bidding on his first donation—the car service. It proved popular. As did the car washing.

Finally the MC said, 'And Nick has added a late entry to the list, and it's very intriguing. Take it away, Nick.'

Nick's gaze speared Blair's. She'd avoided eye

contact for most of the evening, but now that he'd snared her attention he refused to surrender it.

'Most of you won't know this, but I'm in the process of buying a guesthouse just off the Chichester Road. It backs onto the national park, and the property is beautiful. For the auction tonight I'm offering one lucky bidder a room there for a weekend—a beautiful double room in gorgeous surroundings where you can spend two whole days in pampered comfort. What could be more inviting than that?'

Without taking his eyes off Blair, he nodded to the auctioneer to start taking bids. Her delectable mouth had dropped open, her eyes had widened, and her chest rose and fell as if she'd been running. And then she smiled at him.

Parts of him he'd thought dead fired to life. Walk away from her? The notion almost made him laugh. He wasn't walking away. Not without a fight.

'Is that the final bid?'

The auctioneer's demand snapped him to. Blair hadn't made a single bid. *Hell!* He angled in close to the microphone again, snagging Blair's baby blues as he did so.

'Let me just add...' He let his fingers play down

the length of the microphone stand. Her eyes lowered to his fingers. Even from where he stood he saw her convulsive swallow.

He grinned.

She lifted her chin in that haughty ice queen manner she had.

He'd melt this ice queen yet.

'There will be a complimentary bottle of champagne on arrival. French, of course. And…' he raised one suggestive eyebrow '…a spa bath filled with scented oil will be waiting.' What he wouldn't do to see Blair's naked body slicked with oil…flushed with desire. 'Not to mention a roaring fire in an old-fashioned fireplace.'

He almost chuckled out loud when Blair lifted her chin even higher and glared at him.

'Of course all meals will be provided.'

The bidding started up again, fast and furious. Still Blair didn't make a bid. He gritted his teeth in frustration.

'And as a final incentive,' he all but shouted into the microphone, 'I'll offer *myself* as tour guide for the weekend.'

Maisey shot to her feet and made a bid that had the room murmuring. Panic shot through him. Heck! He'd been certain that Blair's curiosity to check out the guesthouse, if nothing else, would have made this offer impossible to resist.

'Going once!' the auctioneer shouted.

Glory whispered something into Blair's ear.

'Going twice!'

Nick held his breath, willing with every atom of his being for Blair to save him. Without haste, and with an innate elegance, Blair pushed her chair back and rose to her feet.

With an insouciance that had his heart thumping in suspense she raised her bidding number...

...and doubled Maisey's bid.

The room gave a collective gasp. There was a pause...and then applause broke out. Nick wanted to punch the air. He didn't. He bowed in her direction and smiled. She shrugged and sat down.

She didn't look at him again, but he didn't care. She was his for an entire weekend. His hands opened and closed as he made his way back to his seat. By the end of that weekend she would be his for good. If he had to use every low-down dirty trick in the book to seduce her he would. Once he'd proved to her that he didn't care what she looked like, that it was her very essence that drew him and that to him she would always be beautiful, then she would finally trust him.

She might be his for an entire weekend, but that didn't stop him from shooting his number up in the air when bidding started on that darn cake. 'Two hundred dollars!'

Every other man in the near vicinity took one look at his face and obviously decided not to mess with him. He sat back down in satisfaction.

An entire weekend plus dessert tonight.

Even that didn't stop him from paying a ridiculously obscene amount of money when Blair's contribution of a one-off custom designed Blair Mac outfit came up for bid. It earned him a squealing hug from Stevie and a disdainful glance of hauteur from Blair herself—ice queen personified.

The challenge fired his blood. He knew exactly how to melt this particular princess. And the minute the music started up he'd get to work on thawing her once and for all.

Blair recognised the determination in Nick's stride as he made his way to where she sat. Something soft and sexy crooned from the speakers. Her pulse chug-chugged. Her knees trembled.

She was dying to be in his arms. There was no point in denying it. She ached to have her body pressed up against his, their thighs and hips moving in time with each other. She wanted to wallow in the seductive sensual promise of what might come later when they were alone…if only she'd let it.

Only…she couldn't let it.

To make love with Nick—even if she could find the courage to bare herself to him and let him see her naked—would be a tacit acknowledgement that they had a future together.

Even if Nick did prove to be the exception—a king among men who could see beyond her scars—it didn't change the fact that he wanted more children. And there was the distinct possibility she couldn't give them to him. Getting pregnant meant going back into hospital. It meant more procedures and more tests. She didn't think she could face that.

She recalled Nick's manner towards the younger kids that day up at the school—his enjoyment, the way his face had softened. He'd been great with them. The life he wanted wasn't a life she dared dream of for herself.

She resolutely ignored the thickening of her throat. She had no time for what-ifs and what-might-have-beens. Whichever way she looked at it, she and Nick did *not* have a future.

'Evening, Blair.'

He stopped in front of her, heart-thumpingly gorgeous in the black tux that complemented the dark sheen of his hair, and the crisp white dress shirt that enhanced his tanned olive skin.

She remembered the way he'd told her they couldn't be friends, and she dragged her gaze from the broad promise of his shoulders to feign boredom. 'Good evening, Nicholas. I hope you're enjoying yourself.'

He'd frightened every other man away from her with his assumed possessiveness. Beneath the table her hands clenched. She'd made her position clear to him!

'Dance with me,' he said softly.

She leant back and raised an eyebrow. 'Is that a request or a demand?'

His brows drew together. He pursed his lips. 'Please, Blair, would you do me the honour of a dance?'

That was when she realised Glory was listening in to their conversation with an avidness that would normally have made Blair laugh. Normally.

She dragged in a breath and smoothed out her face. 'I'd be delighted to,' she said, with as much distant politeness as she could manage.

If only she could manage that same distance when he took her in his arms.

Her pulse fluttered when he took her hand to lead her to the dance floor. Her whole body hummed to life when he pulled her close, curled one hand around her fingers and settled the other in the small of her back, his heat branding her through the thin silk of her dress.

Her body hummed to life, hummed with relief to be so near him, and then it slowly and silently started to scream when he didn't pull her any closer. She was close enough to see the beginning of a shadow on his jaw, close enough to have the spice of his aftershave clog her senses, but far enough away that even the strictest doyens of propriety wouldn't blink an eye. Close enough and yet far enough for her to know exactly what she was missing.

She glanced up to find his dark gaze surveying her with a hunger that almost stopped her heart. His lips were firm and generous, and they promised heaven. His thighs were strong and lean, and she ached to have them pressed against hers. His arms were honed and muscled, and she wanted them to crush her to him.

It was nonsense—all foolish nonsense! He'd put some spell on her to tempt her beyond endurance.

Say something! Break the spell!

She cleared her throat. 'The Miss Showgirl contestants have done the town proud tonight.'

Dark eyes surveyed her. He didn't say anything. Silence settled around them. She couldn't handle the silence, the heat, the promise.

She swallowed. 'You bought the guesthouse?' The words burst from her.

'Contracts were exchanged on Thursday. The lawyers just need to do their thing, and then it's mine.'

'Congratulations. Um…are you excited?'

'Terrified.' And just for a moment it was as it always was between them—right…with an innate understanding and sympathy that needed no words. 'The moment I saw the property I fell in love with it. I saw the life I'd always imagined, and…'

'And?'

'I decided it was a risk worth taking.'

The way he said the word *risk* made her heart slam against her ribs. 'I know you'll make a success of it.'

She tried to look away, but he refused to release her gaze. 'You bid on the weekend away.'

Finally there it was—the thing that was simmering between them.

'And I won,' she said calmly, and hated herself for the lurch her stomach gave as his eyes flared in triumph and possession. 'When Aunt Glory said how divine it sounded, I knew I had to win it for her. It's the perfect thank-you for all her support during these last few months. You make sure you look after her properly, you hear? I want her to have the royal treatment.'

The shock in his eyes didn't give her any pleasure.

'Besides,' she continued, 'I had to save Maisey from the inevitable disappointment of learning of your deep-seated aversion to incense and scooters.' She had no satisfaction in besting him—just a deep burning ache for what couldn't be.

A pulse pounded at the base of his jaw. 'You won't be accompanying your aunt?'

'I'm afraid not.'

His grip on her hand tightened. 'You will join me for dessert later, though, won't you? For a piece of *sachertorte*?'

She remembered her rash words at the auction

table earlier. She'd known Nick had heard her. Half the room had to have heard her. She refused to let her chin fall. 'If you insist.'

His jaw clenched. 'You'd rather not?' he barked.

Her own anger came to her rescue then. 'Damn you, Nick! Did you *really* think you could buy me?'

The air hissed out of his lungs. 'That's not what I was trying to do!'

She winced as his hand crushed hers. He immediately loosened his grip with a curt apology. She didn't say anything. Her heart was thumping so hard it was all she could do to stay upright.

'Hell, Blair, you were flirting with every man in the room!'

'Yes, I was! I was flirting with *everyone*, treating *everyone* the same. And it was light, fun flirting—not throwing myself at the highest bidder flirting! What right did you have to warn everyone off like you've done tonight? I wanted Glory to see me flirting and dancing and getting back into the groove.'

'But you're *not* getting back into the groove, are you?'

'I'm getting back into *my* groove, not yours. I'm taking the steps *I'm* ready for.'

His jaw slackened. It drew her eyes to the shape of his mouth and—

She dragged her gaze away.

'So…' The colour had leached from his face. 'You weren't sending out a signal that you were ready to dive back into the ring?'

'No!' Was that what he'd thought? She had to close her eyes against the temptation that pounded at her. 'I told you how I felt. I told you I wasn't ready for a relationship. I'm sorry, Nicholas, but I haven't changed my mind about that.'

For the first time, though, she wondered at the veracity of her assertion, and the wavering frightened her. It frightened her more than anything had since her treatment.

'It seems to me that we're at a stalemate.' She had no hope of hiding the wobble in her voice. 'I won't be more than friends, and you won't be just friends.'

His face had gone grey. The shutters came down over his eyes and he straightened. 'Thank you for the dance, Blair. It was…enlightening.'

She hadn't realised that the song had come to an end. She opened her mouth, closed it again. There wasn't anything left to say. Nick walked her back to her table and didn't stay to chat. Several moments later two plates of *sachertorte* were placed in front of her and Glory. 'Compliments of Mr Conway,' the waiter said.

And just when Blair didn't think her heart could slump any lower Nick led Maisey out onto the dance floor.

Blair managed precisely two-and-a-half bites of cake for show, before excusing herself to go and powder her nose. Once in the ladies' room she pushed into a cubicle, lowered the lid of the toilet, and sat. She pressed her palms to burning eyes and gulped back tears.

This was for the best. Nick would thank her one day.

He might thank her, but he would never be her friend.

On that thought she had to lift her face, blink, and breathe deeper and harder.

Nick schooled his features when Glory motioned him over after he and Maisey had finished their dance. He straightened his tie and fought the urge to turn and hightail it in the other direction.

Thankfully Blair was nowhere in sight.

He hated himself for even noticing, for caring. The pain that had raked his chest when he'd realised all his assumptions about her had been wrong had nearly doubled him over. What the hell did the woman need to do to get the message through to him—hit him with a sledgehammer?

He'd got it all so wrong, and the pain still cut at him now with sharp jagged edges. He wasn't sure how much longer he could keep a halfway civilised expression on his face. He'd have to leave soon, before he alienated half the town with his bad manners, before he disgraced and embarrassed Stevie.

The moment Glory was finished with him he was leaving, going home.

Alone.

Another shaft of pain sideswiped him. It was all he could do to keep putting one foot in front of the other. Why had he pushed Blair so hard, so soon? *He'd blown it.*

'Don't be a fool,' Glory said without preamble, gesturing for him to take Blair's empty seat.

He sat. He tried to find a trace of Blair's perfume in the air but it eluded him. He glanced at Glory and gave up the pretence. He didn't think he could stand hearing Blair's words repeated all over again.

'Relax, Glory. Blair's already given me the lecture.' He raised an eyebrow, hoped it hid his sense of defeat, the pain that gripped him.

'Well, you are a fool if you let Blair push you away. What is it with you young people?'

Against his better judgement, hope stirred in the pit of his stomach. 'I think Blair is old enough to know what she wants.'

'She wants *you*.'

He leant towards her, his voice low and intense. 'How do you know?'

Glory didn't laugh at him. He doubted he'd care if she did. Where Blair was concerned it seemed he had no pride.

'I know my Blair. I know her as well as you know your Stevie.'

He considered that for a moment, tried to not let his hope or fear interfere with an innate truth.

'She's just too scared to trust her own judgement.'

He remembered then what that rat Adam had done to her.

'I love my niece, Nick. I want to see her happy.'

They had that much in common, then.

He glanced up to find Blair standing by his chair, blinking down at him. He stood and took her hand. 'Glory, will you excuse us?'

'Yes, of course.'

Blair tried to pull her hand free. 'Wait! But—'

Nick didn't let her finish. He tugged her towards the exit. 'We need to talk, and while I'd prefer to do that in private we can do it here in front of everyone if you prefer.'

'We've said everything we can say,' she hissed. But she stopped trying to pull her hand from his.

He caressed her palm with his thumb, and as he felt the tremble travel through her body a wave of tenderness engulfed him. 'Not quite everything, city girl.'

He led her outside into the cool and the dark. He removed his jacket and settled it around her shoulders. 'I haven't told you yet that I love you.'

CHAPTER ELEVEN

BLAIR, trying to adjust to the sudden blast of cold night air, was in the process of tugging Nick's jacket more firmly about her when his words hit her.

She gaped at him. He loved her? She blamed the body warmth captured in his jacket and the musky scent that rose from its folds for slowing her brain.

No, he couldn't.

He loved her?

And just for a moment—a glorious fireworks moment—she thought her body would take flight.

And then she remembered the angry raised scar on her chest, the jagged red against pale skin, and crashed back to earth.

What if he couldn't cope with it? What would she do if he flinched away from her in automatic recoil? *Men are visual creatures.*

She didn't have what it took to go through that. Not again. Not yet. And probably not ever, she finally admitted to herself. Her head was suddenly too heavy for her neck. The effort of holding it up was draining her strength. Her plea for time was simply a foil, a blind, a lie.

'Aren't you going to say something?'

She was finally getting her life back on track. Nick's rejection… She swallowed. A setback like that would have her crawling back into her hole and never coming out.

'Blair?'

The way his voice caught almost had the power to drag her heart from her chest. She glanced around for a park bench or a piece of wall to park herself, her legs threatening to give way at any moment, but the low wall surrounding the town hall's gardens would take her back into the light that spilled from the hall and she much preferred the half-dark. For the life of her she couldn't see a bench anywhere.

And her brain was too fogged with Nick's words to search her memory banks to locate one.

'Blair?'

'Oh, Nicholas.' She pulled his jacket about her more tightly. One of her knees jerked and shook. She braced her other leg and prayed it was strong enough to keep her upright.

'Don't do this, Blair.' He thrust a finger under her nose. 'Don't give me the *I'm sorry* spiel. Take a chance on what you really want.'

What she really wanted was out of reach!

She batted his finger away. 'Stop telling me what to do or how to feel!' He didn't know anything. She dragged in a breath. Yelling wouldn't help either. 'Listen, Nicholas, I am not the right woman for you.'

He widened his stance, hands on hips. His dark eyes glittered in the night, reflecting a thousand stars. Suddenly the dark didn't seem to offer any protection at all.

'Because you can't have children?'

She did her best not to flinch. It was time Nicholas knew the truth on that score. 'I haven't told you this before, but I had eggs harvested prior to my mastectomy.'

He stared. Hope flared in his eyes. 'Then—'

'But the truth is, Nicholas, I'm not sure I'm prepared to put my body through any more medical procedures—even to have a baby.'

He stared at her for a long moment, pursed his lips. 'Why didn't you tell me this before?'

'Because it's private and personal.'

He gripped her chin in his fingers and forced her gaze to his. 'And our kisses weren't?'

She tried to step back, but he held her firm, and heat pooled in places best forgotten. A short while ago she'd sat in the ladies' room trying to stem tears at the pounding sense of loss that had torn through her, at the life closed to her.

If Nick kissed her now…

He let her go. 'So you lied to me.'

Sanity reasserted itself.

She went to deny it, and then lifted her chin. 'I guess I did. By omission. I did not and I *do* not want you pinning any of your hopes on me.' The hurt that flashed across his face was unmistakable, and she had to squeeze her eyes shut for a moment. 'You have to understand that there is no guarantee my body will accept an implanted egg. I'm thirty-six. My body is not what it was even five years ago. There is no guarantee that I could carry a baby full term.'

'Blair, I—'

'No.' She lifted a hand, and then had to grab his jacket as it started to slide off her shoulders. 'I wasn't even going to bother with the procedure, but between them Glory and my doctor convinced me to go ahead with it. It seemed to give Glory some comfort.'

He took her hand, chafed it as if aware of how cold she'd gone. 'Princess, there are no guarantees at all on this earth. But surely the possibility of having a child…even children…is better than no possibility at all?'

She shook her head.

He dropped her hands to grip her shoulders, his eyes intense. 'I'm prepared to put my dreams on hold, to change them for you, because I love you. Hell, Blair, I would rather build a life with you and not have children than have a life with any other woman and have a whole brood of kids.'

Her breath caught in her throat. He couldn't mean that.

'But you…' He gave her a tiny shake. 'You won't even take a risk on really living again, let alone loving.'

His words cut her to the quick. She shrugged out of his grasp. 'And you've come to this conclusion because I've turned you down?'

'I've come to this conclusion because you won't admit what's really in your heart.'

Something in her snapped. He wanted to know

what was really in her heart? 'You just don't get it, do you? Your first assessment of me was correct.'

She slammed her finger into his chest and for one satisfying moment she thought he'd give way, but at the last moment he straightened and tried to take her hand. She snatched it away from him.

'The fact of the matter is that for years—ever since I was eighteen—I have worked in an industry where looks are everything. What I promote—it is harmful. You were right—it's shallow. What I do is shallow. What I am is shallow.'

'What the hell…?'

He slashed a hand through the air and Blair found that it was she who gave way.

'That is just garbage! More nonsense! Look at what you've done for Stevie and Poppy. They've flowered and blossomed. They've grown in confidence. They walk tall. You've given them belief in themselves and now they won't settle for anything less than what they deserve—' He broke off and glared at her. 'I can't tell you how grateful I am to you for that. You've provided a positive role model to all the girls.'

That had been nothing but bluff.

'You are a lot of things—beautiful, maddening,

stubborn, and misguided. But the one thing you aren't is shallow.'

'Yes, I am!' She leapt forward and grabbed the front of his shirt and shook him. 'All that other stuff is a lie! I *am* shallow. I know all the reasons you shouldn't judge someone on their looks, but…'

He didn't try to remove himself from her grasp. He didn't try to touch her. This close to him she could see the gold flecks in his eyes, could sense his silent urging for her to confide in him.

Gulping back a sob, she rested her forehead against his chest for a moment, before lifting her head again. Her hands tightened in the wilting cotton. 'I know I should be grateful that I am alive. I know I should be glad that my body was strong enough to fight the cancer. But all I can see when I close my eyes is how maimed my body is. All I notice is how utterly ugly my scar is.' She shook him one last time. 'I can't even stand to look at my body in a mirror.'

Even in the dark of the night she could see his face had gone pale and still. She released him and took a step back.

'I hate what I look like. If I feel that way, why on earth would I believe that you—or any other man, for that matter—would feel any different?'

He didn't say anything for a long moment. Beneath her dress, Blair's knee went back to shaking and twitching. She breathed hard, as if she'd run a race. Nick barely breathed at all. The silence stretched, sawing on her raw nerves until she thought she might scream.

'You're right, Blair,' he finally said, and suddenly she wanted the awful silence back rather then the dead, emotionless monotone that was now Nick's voice. 'We don't have a future together.'

Those words had claws that tore at her. Even though she knew they were the truth. Her fingers tightened around the fabric of his jacket. She braced her knee doggedly.

'It's not the rest of the world who can't accept your scars and the loss of your breast. It's you. And you're right. We don't have a future together—not until you come to terms with the body you have now. Not until you accept what you look like now and are proud of who and what you are.'

He made something impossible sound inordinately simple.

He reached out as if to touch her cheek, and then dropped his hand as if he'd thought the better of it. 'Goodnight, Blair.'

She couldn't return the farewell. Her throat had closed over.

He turned away. Within five steps the night had swallowed him whole. Blair backed up until the bricks of the town hall's garden bed bit into the backs of her thighs. Her legs buckled. In her mind she heard Glory's voice warn her she'd catch her death of a cold. She leant forward to hug her stomach, unable to keep up the pretence of strength any longer.

If she had bared her scar to Nick and he'd rejected her could that possibly have hurt more than she was hurting now?

She dragged in a breath. That thought was neither here nor there, because she couldn't imagine baring her scar to anyone. She brushed a hand across her eyes and forced herself to straighten, to shrug out from beneath the warmth of Nick's jacket. Bare her scar? She shook her head. She wasn't doing that.

Not to Nick.

Not to anyone.

It wasn't Nick who answered his front door when Blair knocked at five o'clock the following Tuesday afternoon, but Stevie.

'Dad's out,' Stevie said, leading Blair down the hallway.

'Right. Good thing. Probably making himself scarce so we can get down to serious women's business.' She hid her disappointment behind a smile.

When she'd rung Stevie yesterday to make a date to discuss the Blair Mac designer outfit she—Nick—had won, Stevie had asked if Blair would consider making two smaller pieces rather than one outfit. She'd wanted to share her prize with Poppy. Blair had promptly offered to make both of the girls their Miss Showgirl outfits. After all, Nick had paid a king's ransom for the privilege.

Stevie and Poppy's combined squeals and excitement were all the reward she'd needed.

'We collected some magazines,' Poppy said by way of greeting when Blair entered the kitchen.

'Excellent.' She set down the stack of magazines that she'd brought along. The girls immediately pounced on them.

They've flowered and blossomed. They've grown in confidence.

She took a moment to study the two girls as they pored over the pages of the fashion magazines and had to admit that Nick had a point.

'What?' Stevie said, glancing up to find Blair surveying them.

With a smile, she took a seat at the table too. 'I was just wondering what you think is the best thing about taking part in the Miss Showgirl quest.'

'Lots of things.' Stevie bit her lip. 'This is going to sound dumb, but I've really liked experimenting with make-up and hair accessories and things. It's fun.'

'Fashion should be fun,' Blair said slowly, realising as she said it that she believed that and always had.

'But,' Stevie continued, 'making myself do something I'm scared of, and not only surviving it but finding I'm good at it and that people aren't laughing at me. I…that's the best thing.'

Stevie had given a couple of talks—practice, she'd said. One at the nursing home and another to the local Rotary Club. Both talks had been about the importance of community events that involved young people. She'd been fabulous.

'Poppy?'

'Shoes!'

Because of her height, Poppy had avoided heels—but not any more.

'I love shoes! All of them—platforms, stilettos, boots, ballet flats. Discovering shoes has been a dream. I…I don't feel so stupid or self-conscious about being so tall any more.' She grinned. 'I can see now that hunching up makes me look dumb. And that what my mum has been saying for ever is true—that if someone doesn't like me because of my height then they're not worth having as a friend.'

So Stevie and Poppy really did see through all the princess pageantry of the quest to the more important lessons that they could take away with them.

'Though talking jewellery has been divine.' Poppy groaned. 'And catering for the gala night was excellent fun.'

'Getting to know the other girls better has been great too,' Stevie added.

'You know…' Poppy cocked her head to one side. 'I thought the popular girls at school were all really confident and cool, but they're just like us.'

'Bluff!' they all said in unison.

'Right,' Blair said, feeling suddenly lighter. 'Have you both decided on what look you want?'

Yesterday she'd asked them to decide between what she called princess, classic or funky.

'Remember, traditionally Miss Showgirl leans to-wards the princess style,' she'd warned. Though it was becoming clear that the two girls sitting opposite were far from traditional.

'Different is good, right?'

'I think so.'

Stevie took a deep breath. 'Then I thought I'd go for a classic look. I thought I wanted princess, but when I was looking through our magazines I couldn't help feeling that classic was more my style.'

'Good choice,' Blair applauded. 'Poppy?'

Poppy had a tendency to follow wherever Stevie led. Blair waited for her to say classic too.

Poppy swallowed and gripped her hands to-gether. 'Funky.'

Blair tried to hide her surprise.

'I want to wear skyscraper-high wedges and show my mum that I love my height. And I'm figuring that these wedges...' she held up a photo she'd torn from a magazine '...are funky.'

'They're wonderful!' Cork wedges with green satin uppers. All three of them spent a moment drooling over them.

'I'm scared to death, and it freaks me out whenever I think about it too much, but I thought maybe a funky minidress—not *too* short...'

'But enough to make the most of your long legs?'

She nodded.

'Oh, girls!' Blair rubbed her hands together. 'We are going to have some fun.'

After much magazine flicking and diagram-drawing the girls settled on their outfits. Stevie decided on a classic trouser suit with gorgeous flowing lines. Poppy wanted a velvet dress in a print of forest-green, apple-green and cream. It was a courageous decision to step outside the crowd and try something different, and Blair was proud of both of them.

'Okay, I'll draw up some proper sketches tomorrow and get some fabric swatches couriered down from the warehouse in Sydney. Can you girls drop around to Glory's tomorrow after school? You can make a final decision from my sketches then, and Glory and I can take your measurements.'

They set a time, and then the girls raced off to watch some show on television. They invited Blair to join them, but she declined and shooed them off before they missed the beginning of their show, assuring them that she could let herself out. But as she watched them go something twisted inside her. Something painful that brought a knot to her throat. She'd enjoyed this evening. She'd enjoyed the girls' company and now it was almost at a close.

Was she really prepared to give up a chance to have her own children?

The unexpectedness of the question almost knocked her off balance. Her mind became a morass of *what-ifs* and *maybes* that she found impossible to decipher. Swallowing, she gathered up her things, turned…

To find Nick in the doorway.

Her pulse immediately leapt into her throat. She gulped. 'Hello.'

'Hi.'

His eyes were hooded against her and it made her heart burn in protest. 'How are you?'

'Fine.'

He didn't move from the doorway. He didn't invite her to sit. He made no mention of tea. 'I… um…the girls and I have just finished up.'

He didn't say anything. *He wanted her gone!* The realisation slammed her heart against her ribs. 'I was just going.'

With legs that shook she eased past him, walked

down the hallway, and let herself out through the door.

Her legs shook all the way across the yard and out through the gate.

'Why on earth would he *want* you to stay?' she muttered under her breath. 'He told you he loved you and…'

And she hadn't said it back.

Even though it was true.

She halted.

Blair's folder, all the magazines she carried, dropped from her suddenly powerless arms to scatter across the ground in front of her.

She loved Nick.

He loved her.

If she really loved him then…

Her heart pounded and her fingers shook. She found it hard to catch her breath. If she really loved him then his pain should be more important than her pain.

Or her fear.

She sank to her knees. She loved Nick.

It hit her then. She would risk any humiliation for him. Any humiliation.

She leapt to her feet and raced for the gate, almost falling over in her haste. She fumbled with the latch, got a splinter for her trouble…and then she stilled.

She'd put Nick through hell. She hadn't meant to, but that didn't change the facts. Her eyes burned and her throat ached. Words were cheap. After everything she'd done to push him away, why would he believe her? Why on earth would he risk another rejection at her hands?

Very slowly she shook her head. Words would not be enough. She had to find a way to prove to him that she loved him.

Slowly she turned and went back to collect her folder and magazines. Rising again, she made her way home, her feet slow but her mind racing.

Nick found himself twiddling his thumbs and staring up at the kitchen clock. He stopped twiddling to pick up his mug and check its contents.

Empty.

He could relate to that.

With a snap, he set it back down. Enough with the self-pity!

He rose and made more coffee. It would be at least another fifteen minutes before Stevie and Poppy made it back from Blair's class.

Blair's last class. She was returning to the city on Saturday.

He dropped back into his seat at the table and sipped coffee he didn't want. This had to be his third in about an hour. He'd never sleep tonight.

His lips twisted. Then at least tonight he'd have an excuse for tossing, turning and staring wide-eyed up at the ceiling.

He had to fight the urge to get up and race down to the store and force Blair to…

To what? He gulped coffee and burned his throat. To hear him out? She'd already done that, and it hadn't made any difference.

To make her stay?

As if that would do any good. Blair's demons were too big for him to fight. In his heart he knew it was her fight, not his. That didn't stop him from wanting to leap up, find her…and beg her to stay.

He abandoned his mug to rest his head in his hands. He couldn't remember hurting like this when Sonya walked out. He remembered anger and panic, but not this heavy soul ache, the feeling that nothing in this world could ever make him smile again.

With a muttered oath he shot to his feet and

tipped the coffee down the sink. He had to get a grip. If for no other reason than Stevie.

As if his thoughts had conjured her up, Stevie, with Poppy in tow, strolled into the kitchen. He'd been so engrossed in his own thoughts he hadn't heard the front door open.

'Hey!' He did what he could to inject warmth into his voice, enthusiasm. He watched both girls sink into seats at the table and figured he might not have done such a great job on the enthusiasm front.

'Hey, Dad.'

'Hey, Mr C.'

He took one look at their faces and put milk on to warm for hot chocolate.

He hadn't waited up for them because he'd expected trouble. He'd waited up to hear them talk about Blair. They'd talked non-stop about her after her visit on Tuesday afternoon. They'd talked non-stop about her yesterday after their measurement taking and whatnot.

He'd hoped they'd talk non-stop about her class tonight. His gut clenched. 'How was your class?'

'Amazing,' Poppy whispered.

'Awesome,' Stevie said in similar hushed tones.

'So why the glum faces?'

Stevie stiffened. 'We're not glum!'

He raised an eyebrow.

'It's just…'

Poppy tried to pick up the thread. 'We discussed a really serious topic tonight. And my head…it feels…' She trailed off too.

'A serious topic?'

Both girls nodded.

'Are you going to tell me about it?'

They both nodded again. 'But first…'

Stevie's face suddenly looked soft and wistful, young, and a great wave of love engulfed him. He glanced at Poppy and another wave of love hit him. 'Yes?'

'First, Daddy, could we have hot chocolate?'

They needed comfort, warmth, and security. Those were things he could provide. He made the hot chocolate. He dropped three marshmallows into each mug. 'There you go, sweetheart.' He set a mug down in front of his almost grown daughter. 'Drink that up, honey.' He placed another mug in front of Poppy. He took his own mug and sat opposite them.

'So tonight?' he started. 'It was awesome and serious?'

'Blair talked to us about breast cancer.'

He set his mug down before he could drop it.

'Do you know that in the Western world one in three women develop breast cancer, and that it's the second highest killer of Australian women after heart disease?'

He did. Because after Blair had told him that she'd had breast cancer he'd looked it up. He didn't say that to the girls, though. It was obvious they wanted to talk. 'Really?'

'Did you know that Blair had had breast cancer?'

Bile filled his mouth. 'Yes.' He knew there was little rhyme or reason to diseases like cancer, but he'd give anything to have spared Blair going through that.

'You never said,' Stevie whispered.

'I wasn't keeping secrets, girls. I was respecting Blair's privacy. I think it's better that she told you, don't you?'

Stevie thought about that for a moment and then nodded.

'She told us how to do a breast examination so we can check for lumps,' Poppy said.

He knew that the girls' health lessons at school covered the same topic, but obviously Blair's talk had had more impact.

'She's so brave,' she added with a sigh.

'She took off her wig to show us how much her hair has grown after her treatment.'

'And she showed us her false eyelashes and eyebrows. It was amazing.'

'And she showed us how a prosthetic breast fits into a special bra.'

'And she told us how she wants to design clothes for real women now, and not just fashion models.'

'She said life was too short to not give it your absolute best shot. She said we should follow our dreams.'

'Because even if we never reach them at least we know we tried, and that's important.'

He couldn't argue with any of that.

'And she said you should never forget to tell the people you love, that you love them. Daddy, I love you.'

'Mr C, I love you too.'

Nick found he had to swallow before he could speak. He rose and collected both girls in a bear hug. 'I love you, Stevie. I love you, Poppy.' He dropped a kiss each to the tops of their heads.

His heart started to thump. This lecture…pep talk…dose of positive attitude that Blair had given to the girls tonight—did it mean anything? Did it mean that she'd heard what he'd said to her on Saturday night…and that she was going to do something about it?

Did it mean that maybe, just maybe, she was finally ready to take a chance on him?

With a final squeeze he released the girls. 'It certainly sounds as if the class tonight was something else.'

'Totally.'

'I might drop round on Blair tomorrow and thank her.'

'You can't,' Stevie said, reaching for her mug.

'She's gone back to Sydney tonight,' Poppy explained. 'Is it okay if we take our drinks through to the lounge room?'

He nodded, too shell-shocked to do anything else. He fell back into his seat in the now empty, now quiet kitchen.

Blair had returned to Sydney.

Obviously she'd decided to return to her life, to follow those dreams she'd spoken to the girls about.

A life and dreams that didn't include him.

He forced himself to his feet, rinsed out his mug and went to bed. There didn't seem to be anything else to do.

CHAPTER TWELVE

BLAIR pushed the door to her Sydney apartment open with one hip, pulled the key from the lock, and then let it close behind her. She dropped her briefcase and all the folders she carried to the coffee table in the living room and fell back into an overstuffed armchair with a grin.

It was all going to plan!

Her second-in-charge at Blair Mac Designs was over the moon to be offered a partnership in the company. Connie had the vision and the drive to take the company into the future, freeing Blair to…

Follow her heart.

Time for a shower, and then a celebratory glass of wine. Leaping to her feet, she made for her bedroom. Carefully pulling her wig from her head, she went to place it on its stand…and then she halted, turning to stare into her full-length mirror. Throwing the wig onto the bed, she scrutinised her scalp. She had about an inch of hair all over now. It had grown back darker...and thicker.

She straightened and lifted her chin, remembering the daring choices Stevie and Poppy had made in their Miss Showgirl outfits. A buzz cut? She stared into the mirror again, moving her head this way and that. She had the bone structure to carry it off if she dared. Some people thought short hair looked sexy.

Would Nick?

She grabbed up the wig and shoved it in a bottom drawer. If she could have seen her Dana would have shrieked and lectured her on proper wig care. Blair didn't care. From now on she was through with wigs. She had a whole selection of hats and scarves that would shore her up for a cold winter. Hats and scarves that were BC—before cancer.

Averting her gaze from the mirror, she unbuttoned her blouse, kicked off her shoes, and carefully removed her bra and prosthesis.

Until you accept what you look like now...

She stilled. Her fingers shook. Until...?

With a gulp, she forced herself to turn back to the mirror. She took three steps towards it until she stood directly in front of it. She stared right at her chest. The lack of a breast and the raised red scar made her flinch. *This* was her body. *This* was what Nick would see if she ever had the courage to bare herself to him.

And she wanted to—oh, how she wanted to. But… This image—the very idea of it—was what had made Adam run.

Her hands shook. She didn't know this body. It looked so different from how she thought of it, from how it had once been. It was so unfamiliar—alien and deformed and—

A shudder racked her entire frame. She couldn't stand it. She had to look away.

Coward! Counting to three, she forced her eyes back. Her left breast, though small, looked full and round. Her right breast…

Blair glanced from one to the other…back and forth. Healthy left breast. No right breast. Healthy left breast. Big red scary scar. She covered her face. She almost doubled over as pain speared into her. She backed up to collapse onto the side of her bed. And then she seized a pillow, buried her face in it and gave in to the sobs that threatened to swallow her whole.

Eventually the sobs eased. She lay on her back

and stared up at the ceiling, concentrated on regulating her breathing.

A sigh shuddered out of her. Bursting into tears every time she saw her scar was hardly going to be conducive to coming to terms with it. Still, there was no denying that the crying jag had released a whole load of pent-up tension.

She forced herself upright again, pushed her shoulders back. Staring at her scar had filled her with grief, but it hadn't killed her.

Round two.

She made her way back to the mirror. 'Narcissist,' she mocked.

She refused to hesitate, wincing again when her gaze travelled downwards. She reached up and traced the scar. 'Man, that looks like it must've hurt.' She grimaced. It had. But… Her hand flattened against the place her breast had once been. Yeah, the treatment had been hell, but it hadn't killed her.

And she was suddenly and fiercely glad to be alive.

She unzipped her skirt and let it fall to the floor, pulled off her pantyhose and sensible cotton knickers, tossed them aside and then stared at her naked form.

'You have good legs,' she told her reflection. That was something.

She turned and viewed herself from behind. She liked the long, clean line of her back. Her arms were a bit skinny, but—

She planted her hands on her hips and spun back. 'I'm practically bald and I'm missing a breast.'

But her hair would grow back and she could have breast reconstruction down the track. She could do some weight training and build up her arms. She was forging ahead with her plans and following her dreams.

She shrugged, and amazingly she smiled. 'Life could be a lot worse,' she told her reflection, before heading for the bathroom and the promise of a hot shower.

'I'm sorry, Nick, but I have to fly,' Mrs Lamley said, all but tossing the keys of her 1956 Oldsmobile Rocket to him.

'Wait!' he hollered, catching the keys and shooting out from behind the reception desk. 'This is just a straightforward service, right?'

'That's right.'

'Is there anything you're concerned about?'

While he was itching to get his hands on the Oldsmobile, one couldn't be too careful with classic cars.

The white hair bobbed with impatience. 'There's a noise.'

He bit back a groan. 'You couldn't be a bit more specific, could you? Clunking? Grinding? Or—?'

'A squeak,' she said, her hand on his door.

He had to grin then. 'What's the rush?' Normally Mrs Lamley loved to stay and talk about her car.

'Blair Macintyre wants to inspect my premises with a view to leasing them.' She tottered back over on her alarmingly high heels to add, 'Indefinitely.'

Every molecule in Nick's body froze. Blair was back?

'I told her to be there at nine on the dot.'

Considering it was eight-forty-five and Mrs Lamley's shop front was two doors down on the other side of the road, she was in little danger of being late.

If he looked out of his front window in ten minutes' time, would he catch sight of Blair?

His pulse sped up. His skin tingled.

'She's going to open a shop and sell her own designs right here in Dungog. In Dungog! What do you think of that?'

He wasn't a hundred per cent sure what to think, but it was evident what Mrs Lamley expected from him. 'Excellent news,' he managed. 'I'll… uh…' He shuffled his feet. 'Your car will be ready at three.'

'Thank you, Nick.'

The tinkle of the bell above the door as she left sounded celebratory in the sudden quiet. His blood wanted to join in the celebrations, but he did his best to dampen his body's party atmosphere revels.

Blair was back?

He dragged a hand through his hair. She'd been gone for two weeks. They'd been the longest two weeks of his life. But whether she was here in Dungog or living in Sydney it didn't make any difference. She had made it clear where they stood.

Except that seeing her every day, running into her unexpectedly, would be torture.

He rubbed his jaw. He glanced at his watch and then at the front window that bragged a comprehensive view of the main street outside. With a muttered curse he turned and stalked back into his workshop.

* * *

'Hello, Nicholas.'

The voice he'd been aching to hear for the last two weeks called to him now, and Nick made the mistake of trying to sit up, immediately cracking his head on the front bumper of Mrs Lamley's Oldsmobile. He fell back with a curse. Gritting his teeth and feeling like an idiot, he slid out from beneath the car.

Blair's face came into view, a sympathetic grimace twisting her lips. 'Ouch, I bet that hurt. Sorry, I didn't mean to startle you.'

He rubbed his head and rose to his feet, trying not to swear at the pain and the sudden sense of disorientation that heaved through him on seeing Blair.

'What? No laughter, city girl?' he said, before he remembered his promise to keep his distance.

Distance equalled no teasing.

'I remember what happens when a girl laughs at you in your workshop, Mr Greaseball. I'm not risking my best suit.'

For the first time he looked at her properly and the breath whistled between his teeth. 'Looking good, Blair. I've never seen you—'

She wasn't wearing her wig!

He recovered himself. 'Wearing a high-powered suit and dressed to impress. You look like some swish businesswoman.'

Her eyes went wide. 'That's exactly what I am, country boy, when I'm in the city.'

He could believe it. It occurred to him that Blair was a woman used to being in control. The breast cancer must have rocked the very foundations of her world. No wonder she had hated everyone babying and coddling her.

He pointed. 'Your hair—'

'Is short.'

'It's sexy as hell!' His hands itched to run over the spiky shortness, to—'

'Keep your greasy mitts to yourself, country boy.'

She pointed a threatening finger at him, but her lips had turned up and suddenly his chest burned with a need that he already knew Blair had no intention of fulfilling.

'What can I do for you, Blair?'

He bit back a curse when she blinked and her eyes filled with hurt. He hadn't meant to sound so curt or to be so short with her. It was just…

Seeing her and not being able to hold her was torture. It was killing him.

'I was hoping to talk to you. I thought we could do lunch.' She held up a couple of paper bags from the bakery across the road. 'But if you're working through lunch and now isn't convenient then we can make it another time.'

She was already inching away before she'd finished her sentence. In that instant he knew he couldn't let her go. Even if he couldn't touch her or hold her.

'Lunch sounds great. I'm famished,' he lied.

Her relief speared him in the gut. It warmed him. It pulled his skin tight. It made him call himself a hundred different kinds of an idiot.

But he didn't ask her to leave. He gestured to the outdoor furniture. 'I'll go and wash up.'

'I'm sorry,' she said when he joined her, 'but I'm starving.' And without further ado she bit into her pie.

He followed suit, because the only other option was to sit and watch her. That was way too tempting for any man's peace of mind.

And it would be rude, he reminded himself.

'You're looking busy.' She waved a hand at his workshop before patting her mouth with a paper napkin.

Short spiky hair and full plump lips. His mouth dried making it hard to swallow. 'Always,' he choked out.

She folded her arms on top of the wooden table and leant towards him. 'Has the sale gone through on the guesthouse yet? Is it officially yours?'

He couldn't resist her interest, her enthusiasm. 'It has, and it is.'

'Congratulations!'

She beamed at him, and he had to clench his hands to stop from reaching out and touching her. This woman had given him the spur he'd needed to follow through on a long-held dream. She deserved his gratitude, not his resentment, and not him pawing all over her.

'I don't believe I ever thanked you for showing me the guesthouse, but I—'

'Oh, pooh to all that!' She grinned. 'Get down to business and tell me your plans for the place.'

So he did. He told her about the couple he'd found with experience in hotel management who were interested in managing the place for him over the next twelve months while he trained up on the business of eco-tourism. He told her how he'd keep running the workshop during that time, that twelve months would give him time to search for a worthy replacement. He told her his plan to work part-time at both venues until he was ready to take over the reins of the guesthouse full-time.

'It sounds so exciting.'

Her enthusiasm was infectious. 'It is,' he admitted. 'I'm taking it slowly, but I'm comfortable with that.'

'Of course. You have a daughter to consider,' she said, as if that explained everything.

And in a way it did.

He shifted on the seat. 'What about you? Did you sign Mrs Lamley's lease?' Her jaw dropped and he had to laugh. 'That car I brained myself on…?'

'Yes?'

'It's Mrs Lamley's.'

Her laugh warmed him to his marrow. 'Well, yes, I did sign the lease.' She glanced up, her eyes so blue they stole his breath. 'No doubt she told you I'm opening a Blair Mac shop?'

'"Right here in Dungog!"' he mimicked. Then his hands clenched. 'Why, Blair?'

She sat back, her eyes faraway. Then she blinked and leant forward again, eagerness evident in her face. 'I loved making Stevie and Poppy's outfits for Miss Showgirl. It made me realise that I don't do enough of that any more. And I want to.'

'So?' he asked, finding himself leaning forward too.

'So I made my second-in-charge a partner, and she's going to take control of the day-to-day running of Blair Mac Designs while I design and make clothes to my heart's content. We'll need to have quarterly meetings, and I'll need to be in Sydney for Spring Fashion Week and whatnot, but for the rest of it…' She lifted her hands and gave an elegant shrug.

She was back for good! His heart slammed against his ribs. There was a new expression in her eyes. A new confidence.

A new peace.

'And I wanted to thank you.'

He stiffened. 'Me?'

'You challenged me to forge out the life for myself that I really wanted. And I can't remember the last time I've looked forward to a new project with so much enthusiasm.' She grimaced. 'You know, if it hadn't been for the breast cancer I'd still be on that corporate treadmill. *And* I'd probably still be in an unsatisfactory relationship with a complete and utter jerk.' She shuddered. 'Perish the thought.'

It was his jaw that dropped this time. 'Are you saying that your breast cancer was…a blessing?'

'I don't know if I could ever go that far,' she confessed. 'But there has certainly been a rather nice silver lining to that one dark cloud.' She swallowed and straightened. 'So…'

Everything inside him roared to attention, because he sensed that she wasn't finished yet, that she had something important to say. And he didn't know what it would mean.

For him.

For them.

He only sensed that it would mean something big.

'So?'

'So I was wondering if you would like to have dinner with me some time?' She glanced at him and shrugged, lifted a hand as if to brush a strand of hair from her face, and then gave a self-conscious smile when she realised there was no hair to brush back. Her hand trembled before it disappeared back to her lap.

For a moment his mind froze. His city girl was nervous?

'You know,' she added, as if her invitation needed to be clarified, 'like...on a date?'

Blair promptly closed her mouth to prevent herself from babbling. Nick sat across from her with a kind of thunderstruck expression on his face and she didn't know what that meant.

Surprise, no doubt, and...?

Her heart dipped. She didn't blame him for caution and wariness where she was concerned. The one thing she wouldn't do was push him. If he needed time she'd give him time.

She cleared her throat and rose. 'Why don't you think about it and get back to me?'

He shot upright. 'No!'

She swallowed, her heart starting to flat-line. 'Is that no, you don't want to have dinner with me? Or no, you don't need to think about it?' Behind her back she crossed her fingers. Please let it be the second one. *Please let him say he would love to have dinner with me.* Or *like*, she amended silently. She'd settle for like. For now.

'It's a no, don't leave yet.'

Her pulse raced and it became hard to breathe. She sat. With alacrity. It wasn't an outright no, which meant there was still a chance he'd say yes.

She'd fight for that yes, for the chance to prove to him that she was the kind of woman who could return his love completely and without provisos, that she could give herself to him unstintingly.

She would absolutely and positively fight for that.

'You're asking me on a...*date*?' he asked, as if he needed clarification.

'That's right, yes.'

He sat then too, though it was more of a drop, as if his knees had given way. 'Why?'

'I expect for very much the same reasons you asked me out on a date three weeks ago.'

He didn't say anything, but she could see the war that was being waged between his hope and his fear. She sensed his doubt. She'd meant to take things slowly, but now...

She leant across the table towards him. 'Nicholas, may I speak plainly?'

'I wish you would, Blair.'

He mirrored her posture—leaning towards her, his arms folded in front of him on the table, mere inches from hers. His shirtsleeves were rolled up, exposing strong tanned forearms.

She'd always been a sucker for strong arms, and Nick Conway had a pair of the best.

'Blair?'

She shook herself and lifted her gaze. 'I… Nicholas, I love you.'

He didn't move. She wasn't sure what effect she'd expected her words to have on him. She swallowed. She couldn't let the thought that she might have left it too late prevent her from finishing what she'd come here to do.

'I can tell you the exact moment I realised it. I mean, I can't deny that I was attracted to you before then, but—'

'When?' he demanded. 'When did you realise?'

'The night I left here after talking to the girls about their Miss Showgirl outfits.'

His hands clenched, bunching the muscles in his forearms. 'Why didn't you come back and tell me then?'

Had she left it too late? Her mouth dried. 'I almost did.'

'But?'

Her hands started to shake. She gripped them tight in her lap. 'I realised that it wasn't your job to make me feel whole. If I'd told you then I'd have put too much pressure on you. I wouldn't have meant to, but it's what would have happened. It was up to me to feel that I was all in one piece. On my own. Once I'd achieved that then I could come back here and see if…if we still had a chance.'

If her pulse went any faster she thought she might just have a heart attack.

'And do you, Blair? Do you feel whole?'

His eyes were dark and intense, and she suddenly found that she could smile up into them. Because regardless of what he said now—if he accepted or rejected her—at least she had this.

'Yes, I do.'

And then he smiled too, and it felt as if her heart had grown wings. 'So, Nicholas, would you like to have dinner with me some time?'

He shot to his feet. 'To hell with dinner.' He strode around the table, lifted her up, and settled her on his lap. 'I want more than dinner,' he growled. 'I want a lifetime with the woman I love.'

Her breath caught at the possessive gleam in his eye and the uncompromising angle of his jaw. Where his body touched hers—his thighs to her backside, her arm and shoulder against his chest, one of his hands curled at her waist and the other curving around her cheek to the nape of her neck—it heated up and started to throb. Warmth swirled in the pit of her belly…and lower. Her knees started to tremble.

His lips lowered to hers, but he stopped milli-metres away and she couldn't prevent the sound that escaped her throat—an incoherent yearning.

'A *lifetime* with the woman I love,' he repeated. 'Can I have that?'

She nodded. She'd agree to anything if only he'd kiss her! 'Yes,' she breathed.

His lips swooped down, capturing her mouth in a kiss that spoke of frustration, desire, and need. Blair felt as if she was being lifted up on some giant wave and sent hurtling through space with a speed and a force that wouldn't allow her to catch her breath. Sensation pummelled her from every direction until she lost all sense of balance and all she could do was cling to Nick and open up to his questing mouth and his demanding hands.

A mouth that promised her heaven and hands that sent darts of delight dancing along the sur-face of her skin wherever they travelled.

She arched against him, moaned her need as he broke off to press a series of drugging kisses to her neck. One of his hands feathered across her scalp and she gasped as sensation circled out-wards. She shifted against him, impatient and searching.

'I'm going to explode,' she almost sobbed as

her body fired to life under the expert attention of his hands and lips. He seemed to know exactly how to touch her, how to kiss her, how to drive her wild with longing.

He captured her chin between his fingers and his lips took her prisoner again. He plundered her mouth with an intensity and concentration that Blair found she could suddenly match.

She wanted him groaning and trembling.

She slid her hand beneath the buttons of his work shirt to explore the contours of his chest. He shuddered at her touch. His groan when she grazed her palm back and forth against his flat male nipple satisfied her to the pit of her stomach.

His hand snaked beneath her blouse and inched up over her stomach with a tantalising slowness that raised gooseflesh. She pressed herself against it, wanting more of his touch, her body on fire for it. The hand moved higher. A finger traced the line of her bra…and then froze.

Her brain was so fogged with desire it took her a moment to work out why. When comprehension dawned she stilled. And then she sagged against him.

He removed his hand immediately. 'I'm sorry.'

She removed her hand too. 'I'm not.'

His eyes flew back to hers. She bit her lip. 'I mean, that kiss... It was maybe a little more intense than I bargained on.'

He choked back a laugh. 'That's one way of putting it.'

'But I liked it.'

His eyes darkened. 'The moment I touch you, Blair, I'm lost. I don't know how to stop. I lose control.'

She nodded with sudden decision. 'We're never going to be able to take this slow, are we?'

'I'll go as slow as you need me to.'

She wrinkled her nose. She knew he meant it, but... 'The problem is, country boy, that I want you as badly as you want me.'

He grinned. And then he frowned. 'Why do I feel there's a *but* coming?'

She dragged in a breath. 'Nicholas, I've spent the last two weeks coming to terms with my scar—making myself look at it, touch it, becoming familiar with it. You can't commit to anything with me until you've seen it.'

His eyes grew as intense as she'd ever seen them. 'I love your body, Blair, it's true. But it's you, the woman you are, that I'm in love with. I don't care that you have a scar. And I won't care if…if you put on two hundred pounds during the course of the next five years, or if you lose your other breast, or if you have a thousand scars. It won't make me love you any less. Don't you trust that?'

She took his face in her hands. 'My scar is a big thing. I cannot take anyone's reaction to it for granted. Nobody can say how they will react until they've seen it.' She pulled in a deep breath. 'And I need you to see it.' She wouldn't feel easy until he had.

'When?' he asked quietly.

She swallowed. 'No time like the present.' She tried to make her voice cheerful, but her knees had turned to jelly.

Nick touched her cheek. 'You don't need to do this.'

'Yes, I do.'

She'd told him he couldn't take his reaction for granted, and she believed that. But she needed to know she was strong enough to do this too—to show herself to him.

Without another word he set her on her feet, took her hand and led her to the door of his cottage. He kept hold of her hand all the way through the house until they reached the kitchen. 'Will in here be okay?'

It was the one room in his house that she was most familiar with and she was grateful for his tact. He didn't release her hand until she nodded. He checked that the back door was locked and drew the curtains across the window.

Blair gave up pretending that she wasn't nervous. But with a deep breath she started unbuttoning her blouse. Her fingers fumbled with the tiny buttons, but she forced herself to continue. Nick waited silently, patiently. His presence gave her a strange kind of comfort.

With the last button undone, she shrugged out of her blouse and hung it on the back of a chair. And then she reached behind for the clasp of her bra. She paused to ask him if he was ready, and then realised that was completely unnecessary. He was watching her intently, his eyes on her face, as if ready to give her whatever she needed.

In the silence that surrounded them she could hear the gentle tick-tock of the clock on the wall and the call of a magpie somewhere beyond the kitchen window. For a moment her fingers shook too much and her arms lost all their strength. Gathering herself, she unclasped her bra and peeled it away. Nick's eyes never left her face as she gently placed her bra and prosthetic breast onto the table.

Silently she asked him to look.

Very slowly his gaze lowered to her chest. He didn't move, and then his whole frame shuddered as he sucked a giant breath into his lungs. Blair froze as pure, primal fear enveloped her. It froze her to the spot. It froze the tears that burned the backs of her eyes. It froze the sobs in her throat. She made no move to cover herself. Her limbs were frozen. It would have been pointless anyway. There was nowhere to hide.

She waited for him to swing away and slam out of the house. She closed her eyes. It was the only part of her she could move.

They flew open a moment later at a disturbance in the air and a rush of warmth. She found Nick standing directly in front of her.

'You are beautiful.' His voice was hoarse. 'Perfect.'

No!

But the bulge straining at the front of his jeans told her that he was speaking the truth.

He reached out and laid his hand flat over her

scar. She gasped. It was all she could do to stay upright.

'Am I hurting you?'

She shook her head.

His eyes held hers. 'Sweetheart, I'm sorry you had to go through that. I expect it was brutal, but...'

Her heart started to lift. Her shoulders lightened. 'But?'

'If you don't put your shirt back on quick smart, I'm not going to be able to stop myself from dragging you off to the bedroom like some Neanderthal.'

Her eyes widened and a laugh spluttered out of her, and with a whoop she threw herself into his arms.

He caught her effortlessly and swung her around.

She lowered her mouth to his. He kissed her back with an aching sweetness.

'I love you, Nicholas,' she murmured, lifting her head to gaze into his eyes.

'I love you, Blair.'

She hesitated for a moment. 'There's something else we should discuss. Babies...'

He touched his forehead to hers. 'I'll be perfectly content with you and Stevie as my family.'

'But if I wanted to try…' she moistened her lips '…you wouldn't be averse to the idea?'

'Only if that's what you really want, city girl. It's not a decision I think we need to rush into.' His eyes darkened. 'If we have kids, that'd be great. But, Blair, as long as you and I can be together I'll consider myself the luckiest man on the planet.'

She wondered if it were possible for a person to fly. She wrapped her arms more securely around his neck. 'You're going to have to find a new nickname for me, country boy, because this city girl is moving back to the country. For good.'

'Princess?'

She wrinkled her nose.

'Beautiful?'

She beamed at him. 'Better—but I have something even more fitting.'

'Oh, yeah? What's that?' He let her slip down his body inch by delicious inch.

She reached up on tiptoe to kiss him again. 'Lucky,' she whispered.

* * * * *